OTHER TITLES
BY AMY CROSS INCLUDE

1689
American Coven
Angel
Anna's Sister
Annie's Room
Asylum
B&B
Bad News
The Curse of the Langfords
Daisy
The Devil, the Witch and the Whore
Devil's Briar
Eli's Town
Escape From Hotel Necro
The Farm
Grave Girl
The Haunting of Blackwych Grange
The Haunting of Nelson Street
The House Where She Died
I Married a Serial Killer
Little Miss Dead
Mary
One Star
Perfect Little Monsters & Other Stories
Stephen
The Soul Auction
Trill
Ward Z
Wax
You Should Have Seen Her

THE HAUNTING OF THE SARACEN'S HEAD

THE GHOSTS OF ROSE RADCLIFFE BOOK 5

AMY CROSS

This edition
first published by Blackwych Books Ltd
United Kingdom, 2024

Also available in e-book format.

www.amycross.com
www.blackwychbooks.com

CONTENTS

PROLOGUE
page 13

CHAPTER ONE
page 23

CHAPTER TWO
page 33

CHAPTER THREE
page 41

CHAPTER FOUR
page 49

CHAPTER FIVE
page 59

CHAPTER SIX
page 67

CHAPTER SEVEN
page 75

CHAPTER EIGHT
page 83

CHAPTER NINE
page 91

CHAPTER TEN
page 99

CHAPTER ELEVEN
page 107

CHAPTER TWELVE
page 115

CHAPTER THIRTEEN
page 123

CHAPTER FOURTEEN
page 131

CHAPTER FIFTEEN
page 139

CHAPTER SIXTEEN
page 149

CHAPTER SEVENTEEN
page 155

CHAPTER EIGHTEEN
page 163

CHAPTER NINETEEN
page 171

CHAPTER TWENTY
page 179

CHAPTER TWENTY-ONE
page 187

CHAPTER TWENTY-TWO
page 195

CHAPTER TWENTY-THREE
page 203

CHAPTER TWENTY-FOUR
page 211

CHAPTER TWENTY-FIVE
page 219

CHAPTER TWENTY-SIX
page 227

CHAPTER TWENTY-SEVEN
page 235

CHAPTER TWENTY-EIGHT
page 243

CHAPTER TWENTY-NINE
page 251

CHAPTER THIRTY
page 259

THE HAUNTING OF THE SARACEN'S HEAD

PROLOGUE

September 2014...

"WAIT A MINUTE. ARE you telling me that you're an even bigger wimp than you look?"

As soon as she'd hauled open the fragile wooden doors on the pavement, round at the side of the pub, Jessie stopped and turned to see that Taylor was already hanging back.

"Dude, seriously?" she continued.

"I'm not going in there," he replied, looking at the dark hole leading beneath the building. "No way."

"There are steps," she pointed out. "Well,

kind of a slope, but it's the same thing."

"I don't care if there's a gold-plated staircase," he continued, looking up at the dark Saracen's Head sign high above, then turning to the pitch-black window nearby. "It's gone midnight. Let's just go and find someone else to hang out with."

"You're scared."

"I -"

"You're absolutely terrified," she continued with a faint smile.

"It's an abandoned pub!" he pointed out, trying to hide a sense of exasperation. "It's been shut for, like, a year or more. And in case you hadn't noticed, it's creepy as hell!"

"Which is why we should explore," she told him, before crouching down and swinging her legs into the hole. "I told you, I noticed the gate to the cellar was broken and I immediately thought of you. Let's go down there and take a look."

"It's probably full of rats."

"Rats aren't scary."

"Do you have a flashlight?"

"I don't need a flashlight," she told him, before letting out a sigh. "That's the fun part! When was the last time you got to root around in the cellar of some long-abandoned pub? And you know there are stories, right? Loads of people reckon they've sensed something in this place. My dad even said that's the reason it closed. No-one could make it work as a pub because there's just this... *thing* in there."

"You're an idiot," he replied.

"At least I'm an idiot with balls," she said, before lowering herself down into the darkness and starting to shimmy her way down the rough brick slope. "Dude, I'll be telling everyone about this tomorrow. There won't be single soul in town who'll have missed the fact that you're a wimp."

"It's not safe," he complained as he saw her disappearing from view, followed by the sound of her feet pressing on a set of creaking wooden steps. "There's nothing down there anyway except... I don't know, old barrels and pipes and stuff like that."

He heard her calling something back to him, but he couldn't quite make out the words. He looked around and saw that the streets were still deserted, and then he forced himself to step over to the edge of the hatch.

"Jessie?" he said cautiously. "Are you done yet?"

The only response was a bumping sound, followed a few seconds later by a kind of metallic clang.

"This is the dumbest thing ever," he said under his breath.

"It's gross down here!" Jessie called up to him, and now her voice was echoing slightly. "There's, like, cobwebs everywhere. And water! It's like the rain's been getting in and there are puddles all over the place. Damn it, my shoe's already soaked!"

"Another good reason not to go down there," he muttered.

"I found some old barrels," she continued. "It's so cold. There are all these pipes and -"

Suddenly she let out a cry of pain.

"Are you okay?" Taylor asked.

"I banged my head!" she shouted back up at him. "Really hard! The ceiling's so low!"

"It's the cellar of some old pub that probably opened a million years ago," he replied, looking up just as the sign swung slightly in the wind. "What do you expect? The place has been empty for ages, it's probably gonna get turned into flats eventually. Who wants to drink stale beer in some rundown old local when there are way better bars around?"

He looked past the building and saw a few lights in the distance.

"And it's way out at the end of town," he added. "I'm not surprised people didn't want to traipse all the way here when there must be ten other pubs along the way. I know everyone gets sentimental but you can't save *every* pub."

He fell silent as a cold breeze blew down from the seafront, and he shivered slightly as he realized that his evening out with Jessie was turning out to be a dud. He liked hanging out with her but sometimes she got these dumb ideas and he was the only one who ever indulged her. Sometimes he wished that he could just ignore her texts, but he was still slightly hoping that one night he might find some way to impress her. After all, he could tell that she liked him, and he figured that he just needed to make her see that they'd make a good couple. If -

"Are you down here?" she called up to him suddenly.

He looked down into the dark hole.

"What did you say?" he asked.

"Are you down here?" she continued. "Someone just touched my shoulder."

"It was probably a pipe," he suggested. "Or a rat."

"Can you please stop being a dick?" she replied, and now she sounded much more irritated than before. "How did you get back up there so fast?"

"Jessie -"

"I felt your hand, okay?" she continued. "If you were trying to play a trick on me, it's a really lame one. Taylor, do you seriously think you can scare me? I'm unscarable."

"Why would I bother trying to scare you?" he asked under his breath, already tiring of her latest attempt to be edgy. "I don't even think unscarable's a word. Listen, I just want to go somewhere else. *Anywhere* else. There's no -"

"Okay, stop it!" she yelled. "I'm officially done with this shit, Taylor. I'm getting out of here. It's just some dumb cellar with loads of cold puddles and low pipes and -"

Waiting for her to continue, Taylor couldn't help but roll his eyes. From the moment she'd told him about the loose cellar doors and the hatch leading beneath the pub, he'd just wanted to get the whole visit over and done with. He glanced both ways along the street again, worried that some random police car might show up at any moment, and he felt a little surprised that the cellar doors hadn't been fitted with any kind of alarm.

"This is just my luck," he murmured. "Freezing my ass off in the middle of the night. There have *got* to be better ways to spend time in this town."

Looking at the distant lights, he felt for a moment as if he was in danger of wasting his life. He had no idea what he was going to do once he was finished with school, but he knew that further education held no appeal. His dad had offered to set him up with an apprenticeship, but he didn't much fancy becoming an electrician or a plumber or a builder. He wanted adventure and excitement, and he felt fairly sure that neither of those things were going to happen to him while he was messing around in some little Norfolk town. There was a whole world out there waiting to be experienced, and he wanted to grab that world by the horns.

All he needed was a chance.

Just one.

After a few seconds, shivering once more, he looked down into the dark cellar and realized that he hadn't heard from Jessie for a while. He waited, but now he failed to even pick up on any hint of her moving around down there. Part of him figured that she was probably playing some kind of trick, although he couldn't help but worry that she might have managed to get herself into some kind of trouble. As the seconds passed, he felt himself becoming more and more annoyed – yet he wasn't quite ready to admit that he was worried.

"Jessie, can we just get out of here?" he asked finally.

All he heard in response was silence.

"Jessie, I'm tired," he continued. "I don't care what's going on down there, but... if you don't come up right now, I'm going to leave. Okay? Do you want me to just leave you here?"

He waited, but there was still no hint that she might be on her way.

"Jessie, what are you doing?" he went on. "This isn't scary or cool. It's just dumb. And boring. You know how you always complain about people being boring, right? Well, right now *you're* being boring. In fact, if you don't come up right now, I'm just going to walk away. Would you like that?"

Although he wasn't really expecting that strategy to work, he still gave her time to respond before finally stepping back. There was no way he was going to just leave Jessie behind, of course, but he was in the mood to play a few tricks of his own.

"Fine, then," he said, trying to sound as

defiant and certain as possible. "See you later. Give me a call when you climb out and I *might* come and find you."

With that, he turned and walked away, making sure to let his footsteps ring out in the cold dark night. Once he was round the corner, however, he stopped and listened, and he fully expected to hear Jessie clambering back out from the pub's cellar. After a few seconds, however, he furrowed his brow as he realized that there was still no sign of her. He felt as if the pair of them were locked in some kind of stubborn game, with neither of them wanting to be the first to break, but finally he leaned back against the wall and shoved his hands into his pockets.

"Two can play at that game," he whispered under his breath. "I'm *always* the one who breaks, but not this time. This time I'm gonna show you that you're not in charge. I'm the -"

Before he could finish, he heard a bumping sound coming from the hatch. Leaning around the corner, he looked at the open door and realized that Jessie seemed to be running around down in the darkness, almost as if she was starting to -

"Leave me alone!" she suddenly shouted, sounding as if she was in a state of complete panic.

"Don't touch me! Go away!"

"Jessie?" Taylor replied, heading back toward the open cellar door. "What -"

In that moment, before he could get another word out, he heard a terrified scream ringing out from beneath the pub.

"Jessie!" he shouted, looking down into the darkness as the scream continued. "What's going on down there? Jessie, are you okay?"

CHAPTER ONE

Three months later...

"DOES NOBODY CHECK THESE things before they go out?" Jonathan Pearson muttered, standing in the office as he leafed though the latest pre-print. "There are so many errors, I've already lost count by the end of the the first section. There's no way we can send this out to anyone."

"We already printed them," Josie told him.

"How many copies?"

She winced slightly, clearly anticipating his response. "Two hundred."

"Two -"

Turning to her, he felt his heart sink.

"I can re-print them," she said cautiously, "but the budget's kind of running out already and the printer's low on magenta."

"Magenta?"

She nodded.

"We don't need magenta," he pointed out, holding the document up. "We just need black and white."

"But that's not how the printer works," she told him. "Ever since it got hooked up to the net, it needs all the colors to be full or it won't print at all. And the magenta always runs out even though... well, I mean, we never really use magenta. It's a mystery."

"I swear those printers are going to drive me to commit murder one day," he said with a sigh. "Okay, we *have* to do another run, so I'll find some way to make the budget work. Meanwhile, shove these in the recycling and let's just pretend that none of this ever happened."

As the double doors nearby swung open, he turned and saw a man making his way through. Not recognizing the man, however, he turned back to his assistant.

"And let's look into some new printers, shall

we?" he continued. "I swear it shouldn't be this complicated to just print stuff out from a computer. We can land a man on the moon but we can't print out a black and white document if the magenta cartridge is empty. This kind of thing really boils my blood."

"Mr. Pearson?"

Turning, he saw that the man who'd entered the room was now loitering nearby. There was something immediately incongruous about him, and he glanced around the room with an uncomfortable and slightly sweaty stare.

"I'm sorry to interrupt," the man continued nervously, as if he clearly understood that he was intruding, "but I saw your advert and... I think I might need your help."

"Help with what?" Jonathan replied, furrowing his brow as he tried to work out exactly what was happening. "Wait a minute... what advert?"

***

"We talked about this," Rebecca said that evening as she leaned back against the counter in the kitchen. "We agreed that we were going to start looking for cases to investigate."

"Yes, but -"

"After Oxendon we specifically had a conversation about how we need to get more data for our studies. And the only way to get more data is for us to get out in the field and investigate cases of alleged hauntings."

"Yes, I remember, but -"

"So I went ahead and started looking around for something. And I've got to say, this haunted pub sounds like an ideal candidate. It's nearby... ish, it's in a building that has a long and well-established history, and the guy you spoke to sounds like a level-headed person who's not given to making things up."

"Yes, that's all true," he replied, before holding up the little piece of card, "but it still doesn't explain why you put *my* contact details on here."

"I didn't want to put our home address," she admitted, "and the people at the supermarket said that a physical address had to be on the card, so I panicked and put your office details. I couldn't use *my* office because I didn't want anyone there to know what we're up to."

"Oh, but my office is fine," he muttered,

before setting the card down. "And do you really think that a card on a supermarket board is the best place to search for cases?"

"I didn't *just* advertise in the supermarket," she told him. "I also put a card in a couple of newsagent windows around town. The point is, I specifically wanted to find potential cases in unusual locations. I wanted to find people who weren't specifically looking for any help, but who might suddenly realize that they could use a little advice. And to be honest, it sounds like that's exactly what's happening here. So this pub's in Norfolk, right?"

"It's called The Saracen's Head," he explained, "and it's been shut for about a year. Derek Handley and his wife have taken it over and they're getting ready to open it up, but they're worried about certain... stories that have started to spread about the place. And from what he told me today, there seem to have been a few incidents since they moved in."

"What kind of incidents?"

"Nothing too dramatic," he went on, "but enough to make him contact us. Apparently he was in town to visit his sister when he saw the card, and he figured that he might as well get in touch. I've got to admit, my initial assessment was that he seemed to be telling the truth. At least, as much as he understood."

"A haunted pub," she said as she tapped at her phone and started searching for details of the place. Spotting a few images, she enlarged one of them. "It actually looks quite nice. I bet someone who knows what they're doing could turn the place into a nice little local boozer."

"So what's the plan?" he asked. "Are we going to go and bust some ghosts?"

She sighed.

"Marlstone Hall was a mess," he continued. "I nearly died at that lodge, and then the school near your mum's place turned into a total disaster. I'm not sure that we're equipped to go blundering into another potential situation."

"We need data."

"We need to study what we've learned so far."

"We've had plenty of time to do that over the past year."

"We need *more* time."

"When did you become so cautious?" she asked.

He opened his mouth to reply, but at the last

second he remained silent. He knew he'd already lost the argument, but pride meant that he was going to hold out for a little while longer at least.

"The Jonathan I married would have gone storming into a situation like this," she continued, clearly slightly amused by his reaction. "I've already checked and Mum can watch the girls. It's a long drive but we can get to the pub and back in one day, and everything I've heard about the place so far makes it seem like a perfect candidate. We always agreed that eventually we were going to conduct a proper study of a haunted house and this one has dropped into our laps."

"Thanks to a card in a supermarket."

"Are you scared?"

"Scared?" he replied incredulously. "Me? Of a few bumps in the night? After all the stuff we've both been through, do you actually think that I might be scared of a pub?" He sniffed at the idea. "I'm more scared that their real ales might be poorly kept."

"I'm going to go and check this pub out," she told him, "but you don't have to. If you want to stay behind, I'll completely understand."

"And you'll never let me live it down," he pointed out, before taking a moment to ponder his options. "I really don't have much of a choice, do I?"

"That's good," she replied, "because I need you to help me carry the equipment."

"Equipment? What equipment?"

"I've been tinkering in my spare time," she admitted. "I did some research based on everything that happened to us before and I think I might be able to capture evidence of anything we encounter. And that's what we need more than anything, Jonathan. We need proof so that we can go back to a conference and get a better reaction."

"What if we *can't* find proof?" he asked. "What if there's no proof to find? At what point do we give up and accept that the things we experienced before were just... mistakes?"

"Are you losing faith in the project?"

"Faith has nothing to do with it," he told her firmly. "Faith gets in the way of science."

"And sometimes science gets in the way of faith," she pointed out. "Just promise me that you'll keep an open mind. That's what *I'm* trying to do. If we don't find anything at the pub, I'll be the first to admit that we've come up empty handed. But if we end up with some kind of proof, will you be able to honestly acknowledge the fact?"

"You make this sound like the ultimate test," he replied. "Is that how you see it? After our separate encounters at Lotham Lodge and in Oxendon, do you see us teaming up for this Saracen's Head place as the big decider?"

"I see it as a research project in the field," she insisted, "and nothing more. Let's try to not get emotional about the whole thing, Jonathan. The facts are out there waiting in the dark, dank rooms of The Saracen's Head. It's simply our job to bring some light to the situation and determine – once and for all – what's really going on. So how about it? Are you up for a little trip tomorrow?"

CHAPTER TWO

"THE SARACEN'S HEAD?" ROSE said, furrowing her brow as she sat up in bed. "That's a funny name for a place. Why's it called The Saracen's Head?"

"I think it's a reference to the Crusades," Rebecca explained as she folded some clothes and set them on a chair in the corner. "Do you know what the Crusades were?"

Rose thought for a moment before shaking her head.

"They were a time hundreds of years ago when Christians went down to the Middle East to try to reclaim what they saw as the Holy Land. They ended up fighting the locals, and some of those locals were called Saracens. Later on, the same term was used to refer to pirates. It's quite a highly charged name, actually."

"What does that mean?"

"I suppose some people might not like it," she explained as Alicia made her way through from the landing. "You could see it as a symbol of victory over the Saracens, or as a tribute to their bravery."

"Are you talking about the meaning of names again?" Alicia asked as she climbed into bed. "Boring."

"And why's it called a pub?" Rose continued.

"It's short for a public house," Rebecca told her, "which means -"

"Are you two going to talk all night?" Alicia continued. "If you want to do that, then shouldn't Rose have her own room?"

"Your dad and I are thinking about converting the office," Rebecca replied. "Until then -"

"I know, I know," Alicia said, rolling over onto her other side so that her back was turned to both her mother and Rose. "Until then, I have to share. No offense, Rose, but this room really isn't big enough for two of us, especially now that we're getting older."

"I could sleep somewhere else," Rose

suggested softly. "Like the shed?"

"No-one's sleeping in the shed," Rebecca said as she headed to the door. "I know these arrangements aren't perfect, Alicia, but it's not for too much longer. When we get back from this investigation, your dad and I will make clearing out the office a priority and then Rose can have her own room. Doesn't that sound good?"

"Whatever," Alicia murmured, before conspicuously lifting up a pillow and placing it over her head. "I just want to go to sleep. If you two really need to keep talking, can you at least go and do it downstairs? That'd be way more respectful."

"We have a teenager," Rebecca said under her breath, amused by the situation as she turned and smiled at Rose. "Try to get some sleep. My mother'll be here in the morning to keep an eye on the pair of you. You know to behave for her, don't you?"

"Of course," Rose replied brightly. "I wouldn't ever want to cause trouble."

"Can you two please shut up?" Alicia shouted from under the pillow. "Some of us are actually trying to get to sleep!"

***

"We really need to sort out that spare room," Rebecca said the following morning as Jonathan steered the car onto another narrow cobbled street. "The girls can't share for much longer. They're growing up so fast."

"They're not the only ones," he replied. "I'm still not used to the fact that I'm forty now."

"I see it," she told him, nodding at the pub straight ahead. "Wow, they've really done it up. It's so much nice than in the photos."

As soon as Jonathan had parked the car, Rebecca climbed out and began to admire the front of the building. A fresh coat of paint had turned the cracked facade into a stunning white surface while the pub's name had been carefully written out in old-fashioned gold lettering. Each of the windows now had a box with freshly-planted flowers while the upstairs windows – which in the online photos had been boarded up – were now fixed.

"You know," Jonathan said as he stepped out of the car and made his way round to join his wife, "in another life, I think I could have very happily run a pub."

Turning to him, she raised a skeptical eyebrow.

"There's nothing more English than a pub in a quiet little back street," he continued, sounding just a little defensive now. "Open at midday, close at eleven, none of that live music or gastropub rubbish. Just good beer and maybe some basic food."

"And you think you'd be good at running a place like that?"

"I think I'd be brilliant at it."

"What about Andrew?" she asked. "Your buddy Andrew took on a pub a few years ago and it was a complete disaster."

"That's because he did everything wrong," he countered. "He jacked the prices up, he started serving ridiculously expensive food, he chased out all the regulars so he could try to lure the big spenders and the whole thing swung around and bit him on the ass. *My* pub would be calm and quiet, it'd be a place where people go to have a drink and maybe talk a little rubbish for an hour or two."

"You sound like you've given this some thought," she pointed out. "Should I be worried?"

"Everyone's got to retire eventually," he said with a smile. "Why not quit the academic world a few years early and try something different? Come on, Rebecca, I'm sure you'd make a great landlady."

Before she had a chance to tell him just *how* wrong he was, Rebecca heard the pub's front door opening and she turned to see a man wandering out carrying a watering can. He was wearing an old Spurs shirt and a pair of shorts that seemed ill-suited to the slightly chilly weather.

"Mr. Pearson," the man said, seemingly a little shocked to see that he had visitors. "I wasn't expecting you until this afternoon."

"We made good time," Jonathan replied, heading over and shaking his hand before turning and gesturing toward Rebecca. "Derek Handley, this is my wife Rebecca."

"Thank you for coming down," Derek replied, shaking both Jonathan's hand and then Rebecca's before starting to water the plants in various boxes on the windowsills. "We're having our soft opening on Thursday and it'd be good to get all this stuff sorted out by then."

"Exactly what kind of *stuff* are you talking about?" Rebecca asked.

"My wife and I signed on with the brewery a while ago," he explained. "It's a tied pub under Hayes & Storford. They've owned the place for a while but they've always had trouble keeping tenants on. Loads of people fancy the idea of running The Saracen's Head, but they all seem to sour on it after a while. The guy from the brewery didn't exactly say it in so many words, but I got the feeling that even the company has started to wonder if the ghost stories might be true."

"What kind of ghost stories are those?" Rebecca continued.

"Most of them are your usual nonsense," Derek replied. "Don't get me wrong, I'm not against a spooky tale now and again, but I'm not really into the whole ghost thing on a serious level. Most of the previous tenants have reported the odd strange sound in the night and sometimes a knock on a door, and a few of the punters – after they've had some drinks, of course – have mentioned seeing strange figures in the corridor behind the bar. But all that stuff's so cliched and boring. It's like it's been ripped right out of some bog-standard ghost book designed to scare the kids."

Rebecca turned to Jonathan for a moment before looking at Derek again.

"I get the feeling," she said cautiously, "that if that was *all*, you wouldn't have gone to the effort of seeking my husband out."

"Since we signed up, things have been... different," Derek admitted, and for the first time he seemed a little nervous. "Not long before we signed up, some local girl got herself into a spot of bother after she broke into the cellar. She claimed there was something down there. And since my wife and daughter joined me here, we've all noticed that the atmosphere in the pub can change quite quickly. I'm not a superstitious man, but this rubbish is starting to interfere with the business side of things. If I can't get it sorted, my wife's not sure she can hack the whole thing, and without her... I mean, it's a great pub, but it's not viable as a business if my wife won't set foot in the bloody place."

"Mr. Handley wants us to identify the problem," Jonathan added, "and see if we can think of a way to make it go away."

"We can certainly have a look around," Rebecca said as she glanced again at the pub's facade. So far the place looked sunny and distinctly unthreatening. "These haunting cases often have a focus within a building. Mr. Handley, is there any particular part of the pub that seems prone to these ghost stories?"

CHAPTER THREE

"SORRY ABOUT THE FLOOR," Derek said a few minutes later, once he'd led Rebecca and Jonathan down into the cellar. A solitary bulb was just about getting by on the low ceiling. "It's sort of... leaking."

"So I see," Jonathan replied, having to duck down as he passed under a beam. His voice echoed slightly in the gloomy space. "You've got quite the damp problem."

"The brewery are more than aware of that fact," Derek muttered, looking at some of the larger puddles that had gathered in cracks running from wall to wall. "They know about the hole in the roof too. Like I said, we're just tenants so we don't actually own the place. Still, I'd like to think they'll get it fixed before the bloody pub collapses on our heads."

"How often do you have to come down here?" Rebecca asked as she saw stacks of barrels on the far side, each attached to various pipes.

"Depends how often the barrels need changing," Derek told her with a shrug. "The more often, the better. Obviously there's a delivery once a week, so someone has to be down here while the barrels are rolled through that hatch over there. We also use the space as a general storage area, so I reckon someone'll be coming down here at least a couple of times a day."

Stepping over a particularly large puddle, Rebecca walked over to the far wall and looked up at the hatch.

"There seem to be several different rooms down here," Jonathan observed. "Obviously the cellar's a fairly contained part of the larger basement. But this is where the supposed spectral activity is focused?"

"I've got to admit," Derek continued, "it can get... odd down here. Obviously it's cold at the best of times, but every so often the temperature suddenly plummets. I mean, it *really* gets icy. And whenever that happens, there's always this other feeling, like... I can't quite explain it, but it's like there's someone else down here." He glanced back up the steps, as if he wanted to make sure that there was no-one else around to overhear him. "I don't mind admitting," he added, turning to them again but lowering his voice this time, "that once or twice I swear I've heard..."

He hesitated, as if he wasn't sure he could quite bring himself to finish that sentence.

"Footsteps," he added finally.

"And you're sure you're alone at the time?"

"But it's like someone's walking through some of the other rooms down here," he went on, clearly feeling slightly uncomfortable. "Slowly, like, but there's definitely someone there. At first I thought someone was playing a joke on me but the last few times I've made real sure to lock the door behind me when I come down. So then I figured that maybe something was... dripping on the concrete floor, but I don't think it's that either. To be honest, it took a while but I finally came round to my wife's way of thinking. We've both heard a baby crying once or twice as well. Or it seems like that. I don't know, the sound sort of hangs everywhere at once."

"You've mentioned your wife a few times now," Rebecca pointed out. "Is she here right now?"

***

"I'm not setting foot in that place until it's been cleared," Elizabeth Handley said as she sat in a small cafe up on the seafront. "Absolutely not under any circumstances. It's not right."

"You've encountered the same strange footsteps that your husband described?" Rebecca asked.

"Is that what he told you? That it's *just* footsteps?"

Rebecca turned to Jonathan.

"I mean... he also mentioned something about the sound of a baby crying..."

"That's bloody typical, isn't it?" Elizabeth continued. "Footsteps and the crying are the least of it. If it was just footsteps I'd be in there right now. Footsteps don't bother me at all. It's the boy that gets on my wick."

"What boy?" Jonathan asked.

"He didn't mention that, did he?" she replied with a smirk. "Of course not. That's because he knows it's real." She leaned forward a little. "There's a picture on the wall in the main part of the bar. There are lots of pictures, actually, showing the pub over the years. But one of them in particular shows the front of the place back in the nineteenth century, and do you know what you can see standing in the doorway?"

"I can't imagine," Rebecca murmured.

"I'll show you," Elizabeth went on, tapping at her phone before holding up a photo that she'd clearly prepared earlier. "That's him."

Peering at the image, Rebecca saw a sepia-tinted image of the pub's front door, complete with a young boy – clearly only nine or ten years old – standing on the steps and staring back at the camera with a somewhat inscrutable expression on his face.

"I've seen him," Elizabeth added.

"You've seen that exact boy?" Rebecca replied.

"He's downstairs in the pub," the woman explained. "Never upstairs and never in the cellar. Always downstairs, and usually round the area at the bottom of the staircase itself. He doesn't go behind the bar very much. I've done some reading on the internet and I've found other people who've seen him, but no-one seems to know who he was. But sometimes you hear a little laughing sound, and several people have reported seeing a tattered little ball just rolling out of the shadows. He's always got that ball with him."

"He looks fairly well-dressed for the period," Jonathan observed. "Not well-off by any means, but certainly not some street urchin either. And photos were quite rare back then, so his inclusion in this image would have been very deliberate. The most likely explanation is that he was the son of whoever had The Saracen's Head at that time."

"Well, he's still there now," Elizabeth insisted. "I don't know what he wants, but he obviously wants something."

"Children are often linked to the cases we've encountered," Rebecca said under her breath.

"I've only actually seen him once," Elizabeth replied. "I was on my hands and knees, polishing the letterbox on the inside of the front door. I'd got it nice and clean, all sparkling, and I could even see my own reflection. And then I saw him too, standing right behind me. I let out the biggest scream of my life and turned round, but he was already gone. He'd been looking at me, though. Mind you, the place was so dirty when we moved in, I wouldn't be surprised if he was shocked to see anyone bothering to clean it."

"Did you make any attempt to contact him?" Jonathan asked.

"I asked out loud if anyone was around, but I just ended up standing there talking to myself like a total wally." She took a sip of tea. "Then Derek caught me trying to contact the little boy and he started making fun of me, so I told him I wasn't going back to that pub until the ghosts have been sorted out. Jane and I moved in with my sister for a few days down the road."

"Jane's your daughter?"

"If Derek thinks that we're gonna work in that pub when it's haunted, he's got another thing coming," she added, jabbing at the table with a finger. "The man's out of his mind. And if he thinks he can run the place by himself for a while and that eventually Jane and I'll come around, then he's completely deluded." She hesitated for a moment. "So you're the people he called in to help, eh? Don't get me wrong, I'm sure you know what you're doing, but I'd have thought he might go for a priest instead."

"My wife and I have a slightly more scientific approach to these things," Jonathan told her. "We believe that the first step to resolving any kind of problem is identifying the root cause of the issue. Then the second step involves coming up with a plan to tackle that issue, and the final step is implementing that plan in a way that gets results."

"I'm not saying that the little boy's evil," Elizabeth continued, sounding a little more desperate than before. "If you want my guess, I reckon he's probably lost. I feel for him, really I do, but I can't live in that place if I'm scared I might turn round and see him at any point. My heart won't take it. Whatever's going on in that pub, it's real and it needs to stop. Derek won't admit it, but the brewery are running out of patience. They only gave us an initial one year lease, and it's pretty obvious to me that they just want to be able to say that they gave the pub a proper try."

"You think they want to shut it down?"

"It's last orders for The Saracen's Head," she said firmly. "The brewery need Derek to fail so that they can argue that tried their best, and then they'll sell the place to developers. They've got no interest in dealing with that ghostly little boy. Maybe he'll still haunt the place once it becomes flats, maybe he won't, but that won't be their problem once they've collected the money. Pubs are dying in this country and The Saracen's Head is headed for the casualty list. Even if you manage to deal with the ghost problem, I don't give it much hope. That place'll be boarded up again inside of a year."

CHAPTER FOUR

"SHE WAS CHEERY," JONATHAN muttered as he stopped next to the car and looked out across the beach. "I suppose she's got a point, though. Pubs in this country are really struggling."

"No."

Turning, he saw Rebecca watching him with a disapproving expression on her face.

"No?" he replied. "You think they *aren't* struggling?"

"I think they're in a desperate state and things are only going to get worse," she told him, "but that doesn't mean you should be seriously thinking about taking one on."

"I -"

"Darling," she continued, stepping around the car and stopping in front of him, "I love you and

I truly believe that you can do anything you put your mind to. I just don't want to see you get yourself into something that's clearly not going to work."

"I'm not actively looking to run a pub," he replied.

"But I know how these things work," she added with a sigh. "The seed gets into your head and you start imagining yourself standing proudly behind the bar, and then suddenly you're downloading information packs from the brewery website and writing business plans. I just don't want you to get sucked down that rabbit hole, especially not when we're dealing with two young girls at home. One of whom, I'm pretty sure, is fast barreling into that delightful stage of life known as puberty."

"Do you think that's going to be difficult?"

"Alicia hitting puberty?"

He nodded.

"Maybe," she continued. "There's a chance."

"So we need a plan of action for this case," he pointed out, clearly very keen to avoid discussing anything too personal when it came to their daughter – and the fact that she was growing up fast. "I don't know about you, but I don't fancy spending a few hours in a chilly cellar calling out in the hope that some ghostly child answers us. I've had just about enough of that sort of thing."

"Then it's a good job we came prepared."

"We did?"

Smiling, she walked round to the rear of the car and opened the boot. After rifling around inside for a moment, she pulled out a slightly crumpled cardboard box; she opened the box, and finally she lifted up a small metallic box with various wires poking out from one side. The main part of the frame was clearly part of an old toaster that Jonathan vaguely remembered having thrown out a while back, while sections of an old security alarm also appeared to have been scavenged. The overall result was something that reminded him very much of old television shows such as *Bric-a-Brac* and *Blue Peter.*

"What," he said cautiously, "in the name of all that's holy... is that?"

"I've been busy over the past few months," she told him. "I thought about everything that happened at Oxendon last year and I came up with some theories that I've been dying to put to the test. I'm not claiming that I've nailed it first time – far from it – but I'm convinced that this is the first step on the path to developing a method of detecting ghostly presences. If I'm even slightly barking up the right tree, we might be about to make our biggest step forward yet."

"With a magic box?"

"It's not magic," she said firmly. "It's a carefully calibrated device that picks up on changes to certain frequencies. I'm convinced that these frequencies are associated with ghostly manifestations."

"I'm not sure that I follow."

"I'll show you the paperwork later," she added. "Trust me, there's loads of documentation to go with the RP1."

"RP1?"

"Rebecca Pearson One," she pointed out. "I couldn't think of a better name. Anyway, we're getting ahead of ourselves. First, I think it's time for us to put this little bad boy to work. Let's head back to the pub and see if we can find some sign of that ghostly little boy in action."

"Actually, can I meet you there?" he asked. "There's one other little detour I want to make first."

***

One hour later, sitting on a stool in the pub, Rebecca watched as a solitary white light continued to blink on the side of the box.

"Come on, RP1," she muttered under her breath as she opened a panel on the side. "You shouldn't be doing this. You should be spooling up by now. Or did I forget to link that part up?" She peered closer at the various wires inside the frame. "Maybe I should have got some help after all."

"What are you doing?"

Startled, she looked up and saw a young girl standing in the doorway, staring at her.

"I'm... waiting for the light to change," she explained cautiously. "There's a chance I just need to change the bulb. You must be Jane, right?"

The girl nodded.

"How do you feel about your parents taking this place on?" Rebecca continued.

"It's alright, I suppose," Jane murmured, although she was showing a distinct lack of enthusiasm. "It's not like they asked me, anyway."

"You don't like the place?"

"It's creepy," Jane replied. "And old. And dirty. And Dad expects me to work as his cleaner for free. That's clearly gonna be my whole life from now on. Free labor."

"I can see how that's not the most exciting thing in the world. I hope you don't mind if I ask, but have *you* noticed anything odd here since you arrived?"

"Are you talking about the ghost stuff?" Raising a skeptical eyebrow, Jane hesitated before making her way over to take a closer look at the box on the bar. "Of course you are. That's all Mum and Dad argue about these days."

"Your mother thinks there's a ghostly boy in

the pub."

"Oh yeah," she said with a faint smirk. "You mean the one that rolls his ghostly ball along?"

"Have you witnessed anything like that?"

"Mum reads way too many of those stupid magazines," Jane explained. "I don't know if there are any ghosts here, but even if there weren't, Mum would still be going on about them. She's got it into her head that the boy from that photo is somehow haunting the place."

Turning, Rebecca saw the photo of the young boy; earlier she'd seen the image on Elizabeth's phone, but now she saw a framed copy sitting next to several other pictures from the pub's past. This copy was a little clearer, and she couldn't help but notice now that the boy was indeed holding what appeared to be a small ball in his left hand.

"Anyway, it's not this part of the place that's creepy," Jane explained. "It's totally the cellar. Any idiot knows that."

"Has anything happened to you down there?"

"I... don't know," Jane replied, as if she was nervous about what she might say next.

"You can tell me," Rebecca insisted. "I'm here to help."

"With your blinking box?"

"It's taking a little time to get going."

"I mean, I've felt weird in the cellar a bunch

of times," Jane explained. "Sometimes it's like there's someone there even though you can't see them, and then this one afternoon..."

Her voice trailed off.

"What happened?" Rebecca asked.

"Don't tell my dad this," Jane continued, "but I felt someone touch me. Like, I swear an actual hand brushed against me." She demonstrated, running her hand briefly across her belly. "Just like that. It was quick but... it felt so real."

"Have you told anyone else about it?"

Jane shook her head.

"Not even your parents?"

"And add even more fuel to the fire?" she replied, clearly repulsed by the idea. "No way. Mum and Dad are at each other's throats loads as it is. It's bad enough that she's moved me and her out to my aunt's house. Whatever happened to me in the basement was probably nothing, but it was creepy enough to make me avoid going down there as much as possible. Which isn't exactly easy now that Dad insists on storing all the cleaning supplies down there, which means that I have to go down at least twice every single day."

She looked at the box.

"It hasn't changed," she pointed out.

"It takes time."

"To do what?"

"To pick up on changes in different

frequencies," Rebecca explained, trying not to sound too defensive. "It's kind of complicated and it's only at a very early stage. And to be honest, I'm not even certain that it's going to work at all. I'll probably need to test it a whole load of times before I'm able to fine tune it enough."

"But you think ghosts are real, right? I mean, you seem kinda smart, so I'm thinking that you probably have a better idea about the whole thing."

"I think we need to explore the subject extremely carefully."

"But you've seen one? A ghost, I mean. Have you actually..."

Her voice trailed off and she let the question hang in the air for a moment.

"I've seen enough to pique my curiosity," Rebecca admitted finally, taking great care to choose only the most appropriate words. "I get it, your parents are probably too worried about their business to step back and see things properly. If you want to tell me anything, anything at all, I'll listen in complete confidence."

Jane hesitated again, as if she was about to say something. At the last second, however, they both heard the pub's back door swinging open – followed by the sound of Derek huffing and puffing to himself.

"It wasn't a child," Jane said, stepping back

and hurrying back across the room. "The hand. I could tell it wasn't a child. I don't know anything else."

Rebecca opened her mouth to ask exactly what she meant, but Jane was already gone. Hearing Derek's voice calling out, asking his daughter for help, Rebecca could only sit in silence as the metal box on the bar continued to blink impotently. And then, a moment later, she looked down at the floorboards as she realized that she might be wasting her time in the bar itself.

The real mystery of The Saracen's Head certainly seemed to exist not in the bar but in the cellar below.

AMY CROSS

CHAPTER FIVE

"I'M SORRY AGAIN FOR disturbing you like this," Jonathan said as he stepped into the cottage's front room. "I found a news report about the incident and looked online and... well, I was lucky to find your address."

"Normally I wouldn't just let a stranger in like this," Daphne replied, "but... to be honest with you, right now I'll take anything that might wake her up a bit."

Stopping in the doorway, Jonathan immediately saw the young girl sitting slumped in a chair.

"Jessie has barely spoken since that night at The Saracen's Head," Daphne explained. "Her physical injuries are all healed, but it's as if she just doesn't want to talk to anyone. She's seen some therapists and she managed a few words with them, and the doctors don't think there's anything actually wrong in her head, but she just... she sits there and stares into space all day and all night. She barely even eats or sleeps."

She paused to sniff back tears before turning to him again.

"I'm sorry, what did you say you were doing here again?"

"I'm a researcher," he replied, pulling out the badge he used to enter various university buildings. "Sorry, I know it's not quite as flash as a police I.D. but I'm afraid it's all I've got. My wife and I are investigating The Saracen's Head and, well, I wanted to speak to Jessie about everything that happened to her down in that cellar."

"Be my guest," Daphne said, turning and heading through to the kitchen. "I don't mind admitting, I'm at the end of my tether. Be gentle with her, though. I'll see about fixing that cup of tea for you. Is Earl Grey okay?"

Once Daphne was gone, Jonathan cautiously made his way across the room until he was standing next to the chair. At first he felt hesitant to break the silence, and he was certainly very much aware of a strange tension that seemed somehow to be hanging in the air. More than anything, he could tell that this tension – and the silence that came with it – was apparently emanating entirely from the young girl herself, as if she was somehow projecting her own internal attempts to stay calm. Yet he'd traveled too far now to simply respect that silence and turn around.

"Hi, Jessie," he said finally. "I'm Doctor Jonathan Pearson and I'd like to ask you a few questions about the accident you suffered a while back. I know the basics, I know you were down in the cellar of the pub and you were sort of... rooting about in the darkness."

He waited for a reply, but she was still just staring at the window. After a moment he took a seat in one of the other chairs, and as he saw the girl's face properly for the first time he couldn't help but notice that she seemed very pale. Several months had passed since her strange encounter in the pub's cellar, yet the terrified scream had apparently not quite faded away just yet.

"Don't worry," he continued, "you're not in trouble. It's more the fact that I think you might be able to help me. From what your mother said when I came in, I get the feeling that people don't really believe you when you tell them what happened in that cellar. The thing is, I'm willing to listen to you with an open mind. I want to know -"

Before he could finish, her eyes flicked with a clicking sound until she was staring at him. The rest of her body, however remained entirely motionless.

"O... kay," he said, determined to seem unflustered. "I'm glad to have your attention, Jessie. I can call you that, can't I?"

He waited, but she was simply continuing to stare at him.

"I want to know what's in that basement," he said firmly. "If you have any idea -"

"Have you been in there?" she asked, and her voice sounded unusually harsh, almost damaged.

"Briefly," he explained, "but -"

"Stay out!" she snarled through gritted teeth. "Do you understand me? Don't go down there, especially not alone! You can't let her hurt anyone else!"

***

As soon as she pulled the cord, the solitary bulb flickered back to life and Rebecca found herself once again looking out across the pub's low, cramped cellar.

Some kind of machinery over by the barrels was emitting a very faint buzzing sound, but as she stepped away from the bottom of the stairs and tried to avoid the puddles Rebecca was struck by the overall stillness of the space. In fact, as she stopped next to a low stone archway, she realized that she could just as easily be looking at a photograph of a room, since the entire cellar appeared to be almost frozen in time.

And then, as she took another step forward, the ground shifted slightly beneath her feet.

Looking down, she saw that the concrete floor in this part of the cellar was in such a poor state that several chunks had separated from the rest. She pushed down a little harder with her right foot and saw one of the concrete sections sinking a little, accompanied by a bubbling sound. Whatever was beneath the cellar, she realized in that moment, was clearly extremely soggy – and hardly conducive to structural integrity.

"Talk about a damp problem," she said under her breath as she picked her way carefully over to the barrels.

Although she didn't really understand how the system worked, she was able to deduce that lines ran up from the barrels and into the ceiling, and that from there they most likely wriggled their way through the centuries-old building until reaching the pumps on the bar. The barrels themselves were large and silver, and when she touched one she immediately felt that its metallic side was surprisingly cold. Several other barrels had been left nearby, no doubt waiting to be changed over and put into service once their predecessors had been emptied by thirsty customers.

And if -

Suddenly hearing a scuffing sound, she turned and looked toward an arched doorway nearby. She saw only darkness on the other side, but already her heart was racing as she began to wonder whether she might have company.

"Is anyone there?" she called out. "Derek? Jane? If someone's down here, can you let me know so that I don't waste time chasing after shadows?"

She waited, but deep down she was already fairly sure that the others were all upstairs. As much as she didn't want to overreact, she was starting to feel more and more certain that some kind of presence was inhabiting the pub's cellar, and a moment later she walked over to the arched doorway and pulled a flashlight from her pocket.

After switching the flashlight on, she aimed the beam through into what turned out to be a small and somewhat dirty little room that had clearly been used for the storage of junk.

"I don't know about you," she remembered Jonathan having said earlier, "but I don't fancy spending a few hours in a chilly cellar calling out in the hope that some ghostly child answers us. I've had just about enough of that sort of thing." Yet that, Rebecca realized now, was exactly what she'd ended up doing.

"No sign of anyone so far," she muttered, before stepping into the next room and making her way to the doorway on the far side.

Shining the flashlight into the next part of the basement, she saw a larger and much emptier room. The floor in this part of the building was in slightly better condition, and as she stepped forward Rebecca felt as if the entire basement level of the building was a hodgepodge of different spaces that had been simply left to fester over the years. Sure, the main cellar area had been updated in order to keep the pub running, but for the most part the space beneath the pub had been completely forgotten by successive owners and tenants.

The only sign of life in this part of the space was a solitary spider that slowly stretched as it continued to hang from a nearby web.

"I bet you don't get much luck down here," Rebecca told the spider as she ducked past and walked across the space, with her footsteps echoing loudly. "I'm not even sure that -"

Suddenly she heard a second set of footsteps approaching loudly. Stopping, she barely had time to even realize what was happening before something brushed against her shoulder. She instinctively turned, and already the footsteps were marching further away through the cellar.

"Who's there?" she called out, but now the sound had faded to nothing.

Reaching up, she touched her shoulder. She had no doubt whatsoever that there had definitely been something nearby, and that this particular 'something' had definitely touched her as it made its way past. She was also certain that she hadn't actually seen anyone or anything, which meant that the presence had somehow existed on some other level. As much as she knew that she needed to stay calm and that she had to avoid jumping to too many assumptions, she couldn't help but think that she'd just made first contact with whatever spirit had taken up residence in the pub's cellar.

Or, rather, the spirit had been the one to make contact with *her.*

"I know you're down here," she said finally, determined to break the impasse. "How about we cut the whole guessing game out entirely, huh? I could wander around calling out to you for a while, but what's the point? If you're here, then you might as well just show yourself. I'm not just here to help the people upstairs. If it's at all possible, I'd also like to help you as well."

She waited, watching the gloomy space ahead, completely unaware that a dark shadow was slowly spreading across the wall directly behind her.

CHAPTER SIX

"AT FIRST I THOUGHT it was Taylor," Jessie said, and now her voice was trembling with fear as she recalled her night in the cellar of The Saracen's Head. "He's not exactly known for his pranks but... I thought he'd finally found a way to freak me out."

"Taylor's your friend, right?"

"*Was* my friend," she replied, correcting him. "But after a couple of minutes I realized that there was something else down there with me, something that... I want to say following me, but it wasn't quite like that. It was keeping pace with me, and I know it was watching me, but I almost felt like I was being..."

She hesitated, trying to find the right word.

"Hunted," she added finally.

"By a person?"

"By something," she continued. "After a while I got lost. It's like a maze down there, there are all these little rooms and the ceiling's so low. I kept banging my head on pipes, and to be honest I started to get kinda scared. I know how stupid that sounds, but I guess I can get kinda claustrophobic and I wasn't sure I'd ever find my way out. I would've used my phone for light, but of course my mum had kept calling me all day about dumb stuff so I was out of battery. I keep telling her not to phone me unless it's for something important but she never listens."

"And then you encountered something?"

"Eventually I stopped," she explained. "Like, I wanted to get my bearings, so I found this corner and I stopped. And I listened. And that's when I heard her."

"Her?"

"It was a woman," she told him. "I don't even know how I know that, I just... I just do, okay? It's not like I could hear her breathing, it was quieter than that. Like, it was totally more subtle. It was like I could hear every time she moved. It was like she was all stiff and her joints just... creaked."

"I believe that's called getting old," he replied, trying to lighten the mood a little with a joke.

"It was pitch black down there but she was staring at me," she went on. "Again, I don't know how I know, I just... I know. And I knew then, too. I knew I had to get the hell out of there but I didn't know which way to go, and I was scared that she might try to stop me. I heard Taylor calling out a few times and I thought I could try to follow his voice, but I swear I was just... frozen in place. Like I was too scared to even move."

"Is that when you screamed?"

She turned to him.

"My understanding," he continued, "is that you screamed, and that's when your friend went and called for help. Someone turned up with a key and they found you on the floor in the cellar, curled into a ball in the fetal position and shaking. You must have been down there for a good half hour before you were rescued, Jessie. If you don't mind a few more questions... between the scream and the moment when someone turned the lights on and helped you out of there, what exactly happened?"

She hesitated again, before slowly shaking her head.

"I'm a researcher," he reminded her. "I won't laugh or make fun of you and I won't spread anything you say around. I just want to know the facts as you understand them."

"She wouldn't leave me alone," she said as tears began to fill her eyes.

"What did she say to you?"

"Say?" She shook her head. "She didn't *say*

anything."

"Then what -"

"It was here," she continued, reaching down and placing one hand against her belly. "She was standing over me in the dark, and I swear... she reached down and she kept touching me right here."

***

Struggling a little to get past a particularly large puddle, Rebecca finally had to jump away from the doorway. Steadying herself against the cracked wall, she stopped for a moment in another room of the pub's labyrinthine basement. She could smell dampness in the air, and every so often she heard a faint but slightly ominous dripping sound coming from somewhere unseen.

"So this is how you're going to play it, huh?" she continued, hoping to perhaps find some way to goad the ghostly figure out of hiding. "Don't you think it's a bit cliched? If you're here and you can hear me, why don't you just appear for a little chat?"

She fell silent for a moment, but again all she heard was a series of drips. Looking down, she saw the cracked concrete floor again and she couldn't help but wonder whether one day the entire pub was simply going to sink down into whatever boggy ground was bubbling away beneath the building.

"This doesn't seem like much of a place to hang out," she went on. "Don't you ever leave the cellar? Not even for a short break?"

As those last words left her lips, the dripping sound briefly became a little faster – and perhaps slightly louder too. For a moment Rebecca couldn't help but wonder whether this was in some way intended as a response to her questions, although she quickly reminded herself that most likely it was simply a sound caused by the pub's immense structural problems.

"It's almost like you're trapped here," she pointed out. "Is that it? I'm still trying to understand how these things work, but are you trapped here by some -"

In that moment a single footstep rang out. Turning, she looked back the way she'd just walked; the sound had already faded, but she felt sure that she'd heard a single and very distinct step, as if someone had placed a foot against the ground and had then frozen.

"You're not the boy from upstairs," she continued. "I'm pretty sure of that. But you might know him. And unless I'm very much mistaken, it takes quite a bit of effort for someone to stick around a place after they're dead. So there has to be a reason for you to be here in this... cracked and rundown place. I've got to admit, if it was me, I'm pretty sure I'd have left by now."

She turned and looked in the other direction.

"But not you," she added. "You stick around and -"

Before she could finish, she heard more footsteps, this time seemingly marching through one of the basement's other rooms. She hurried to the next doorway, looking into the main cellar area, and in that instant the footsteps stopped abruptly somewhere near the barrels.

"Are you trying to lead me somewhere?" she asked. "Are you trying to show me something?"

Walking over to the barrels, she realized that she was more or less exactly back where she'd started. She looked at the various pipes running from the different barrels, but nothing about the sight seemed even remotely unusual and she found herself struggling to believe that some ghostly entity would be haunting the cellar purely because of the beer choice. Still, she had to admit that this part of the cellar was clearly the focal point for the strange activity, and she also had to admit that there was now no doubt that *something* was present.

She knew Jonathan might well push back a little, but she felt confident enough to declare that The Saracen's Head was most definitely haunted.

She just -

Suddenly she felt something brushing against her belly. Startled, she resisted the urge to pull away and instead she looked down. She saw nothing untoward, yet for a few seconds she couldn't shake the strange sensation that in some way a hand was touching her just above her waist.

As much as she wanted to believe that she was wrong, the sensation persisted until she began to feel distinctly uneasy.

"Who are you?" she asked, unable to quite hide the sense of panic that even now was starting to spread through her voice. "What do you want?"

She waited, but the hand was still there – and she was starting to feel more and more uneasy with each passing second.

"What do you want?" she asked again, taking a step back and instantly feeling the hand starting to fade away.

As her right foot pushed down against another loose section of concrete on the floor, she turned and looked back across the gloomy cellar.

"Who -"

"Alexander," a woman's voice whispered suddenly, breaking through the otherwise silent damp air.

Rebecca immediately opened her mouth to reply, but in that second she felt a shiver of shock run through her chest. She told herself that she had to be wrong, yet her heart was racing and she already knew without any doubt whatsoever that the voice had been real. And it had said *his* name.

AMY CROSS

CHAPTER SEVEN

"THAT... ISN'T POSSIBLE," JONATHAN said about an hour later as he sat with Rebecca in the pub's restaurant area. "I need you to be really logical about this. There's no way that -"

"She said his name," Rebecca replied through gritted teeth. "Why would I make this up? Of all the things -"

"I'm not saying for one second that you'd make it up," he told her, reaching out and taking hold of her hand. "That possibility never even occurred to me. It's just -"

"She said Alexander," she continued, "and she put her hand on my belly."

He opened his mouth to reply, but at the last second he sighed and sat back. Looking around, he tried to think of some way to explain his wife's claims, although finally he realized that there was really only one option left. He knew he had to be extremely careful, and that even the slightest miscommunication could cause an argument, but at the end of the day he felt he also had a duty to try to calm things down.

"It's a coincidence, then," he muttered. "It's one big coincidence, and you have to put your emotional reaction aside and remember that we're researchers first and foremost. We can't let our personal lives influence our work."

"There's no way this is a coincidence," she told him. "That thing in the basement knows about _"

Before she could finish, she heard a bumping sound out in the hallway. She turned just in time to see Jane carrying a mop and bucket past the open door; she waited until the girl was out in the garden before turning to her husband again.

"It knew about Alexander," she added. "Somehow she knew that we had a child named Alexander. She touched my belly. Even Alicia doesn't know she once had an older brother."

"She didn't -"

Again Jonathan stopped himself just in time.

"He was still her brother," she murmured, "even if he died before he could be born. I know we usually tell people that we only ever had one child, because it's just easier to avoid the questions, but I carried him for six months. And I know you thought it was a bad idea to give him a name, but I couldn't help it. And now that *thing* in the cellar somehow read my mind or read my history, and she specifically said his name." She paused. "This is about children."

"You're making quite a big assumption."

"No, I'm really not," she continued. "Think about it. Marlstone Hall was about children, and so was Oxendon. Okay, there was no obvious link to children at that lodge you went to, but there are always going to be exceptions. I know how crazy it sounds and I know I need more evidence to back up my claims, but children are the key to most of these hauntings."

"Rebecca -"

"And let's not forget Rose."

"What about Rose?"

"She's a child too," she pointed out, "and she has some kind of connection to the world of ghosts. You can't deny it. You even did all those tests to try to prove it, and you *did* find some kind of correlation."

"I'm still trying to devise more tests about that," he admitted somewhat grumpily.

"I'm not pretending that I understand every aspect of it," she continued, "but I'm certain that I'm onto something. My device on the bar didn't pick up a damn thing while I was in the cellar, but that doesn't mean I've given up on it."

"Why do I get the feeling that we're not going to be getting out of here anytime soon?" he asked, sounding more than a little tired.

"I've got a few more things in the car," she told him. "You can do what you want, Jonathan, but I'm staying until I make contact with this entity properly. She knew about Alexander. That has to mean something."

***

Having gathered for a few minutes at the top of the wall, the drip finally fell and landed with a brief plopping sound in a puddle over by the wall.

"Twenty-one," Jonathan said, making little effort to hide a sense of boredom as he watched the ripples slowly fading away. "One every four minutes, more or less. Obviously the moisture from the ground level is leaking through and meeting whatever's coming up from beneath the building. No surveyor worth their salt would ever sign this place off. Jokes aside, it really *might* come crashing down at some point."

Realizing that Rebecca still hadn't said anything, he turned to see that she was still adjusting some dials on the front of her latest homemade device.

"What exactly does that thing do again?" he

asked.

"It's designed to sense electromagnetic changes," she replied. "I call it the RP5."

"RP5?" He paused. "What happened to the RP2 to RP4?"

"They were... duds," she admitted. "It's a little too complicated to explain right now."

"Oh, sure," he said, raising both eyebrows at once. "Forgive me for asking. I couldn't possibly understand."

She turned to him.

"You don't have to humor me," she said, clearly slightly annoyed by his tone. "Mum doesn't mind looking after the girls overnight but you can still head home and take them off her hands."

"And leave you here?"

He paused for a moment, watching as she got back to work. He wasn't sure, but he was starting to think that her hand might be trembling slightly.

"You know, I still think about him too," he continued finally. "About Alexander, I mean. I don't mention him ever, but that's because I don't want to upset you. But sometimes I catch myself wondering what our lives would have been like if we'd had two kids. Two kids who survived, I mean. Alicia certainly would have had a very different experience."

"Alicia doesn't know anything about him,"

she said firmly. "We agreed that we weren't going to tell her."

"That doesn't mean she shouldn't *ever* find out," he countered. "The miscarriage -"

"Can we just drop it, please?" she asked, cutting him off. "You're the one who was lecturing me about keeping emotion out of the investigation earlier. I'm trying to stay focused, but it's difficult if you keep bringing up the past."

"Point taken," he muttered, before checking his watch. "So how do these various devices work, anyway? If a ghost wanders past, will some kind of alarm go off?"

"There are various sensors that provide real-time information," she told him, "and later I can download a more comprehensive log from the onboard hard drive. I know it might not look like much, but I actually think that I did quite a good job. Obviously it's little more than a prototype, but I tested it out a few times and now we're in the field so... well, I'm confident that with some additional fine-tuning it's going to work eventually."

Hearing the floorboards creaking in the room above, Jonathan looked up at the ceiling.

"I know Derek said it's okay for us to stay the night," he said as he slowly got to his feet, "but I'd better run through the details with him one more time."

Wincing as he felt a slight pain in the small

of his back, he made his way to the stairs. Once again realizing that Rebecca hadn't responded, he turned and saw that she was still fiddling with her latest device; for a few seconds he could only watch as he tried to think of something to say that might make her feel a little better. He hated the idea that she might be reliving the nightmare of their son's death, but deep down he knew that anything he said to her in that moment would only make things so much worse.

"I'll be upstairs," he continued finally. "Do you want to come up in a little while and we can go through our plans for this evening? And then do you want to figure out where we're going to go for dinner?"

"Sure," she murmured. "Whatever."

"Whatever," he said, wincing again as he began to make his way up to the bar.

Once her husband was gone, Rebecca continued to sit working patiently for a few seconds. As soon as she heard the door at the top of the stairs creaking shut, however, she turned and looked across the cellar; she waited, and sure enough soon heard the sound of Jonathan and Derek talking upstairs, and she knew that the landlord's daughter was likely out somewhere in the town. As soon as she was sure that she wasn't going to be disturbed, then, she set the device down and pulled one of her bags closer.

Reaching inside, she fumbled briefly before pulling out a board. She shifted around on her stool and set the board down before opening it out, revealing a spirit board complete with the numbers zero to ten plus all the letters of the alphabet – and the words Yes and No in the middle.

"Sorry, Jonathan," she said under her breath, taking out a planchette. "I know you'd never approve of anything so unscientific, but I *have* to make contact with this entity. I need to find out exactly what she knows about Alexander."

CHAPTER EIGHT

"MARGARET PARSONS," REBECCA WHISPERED out loud after scrolling down the website a little further and seeing the name of the landlady who'd lived at The Saracen's Head from 1856 to 1858. "How about you? Are you here? Can you hear me?"

She waited, with a fingertip holding the planchette against the board, but once again she felt no hint of a reply. She'd been steadily going through every female name she could find on the list of former licensees at the pub, hoping that eventually she might be able to hit upon whoever was now haunting the cellar. So far, however, she'd had no luck at all and her biggest concern was that at some point Jonathan might sneak down and catch her in the act.

She knew that a spirit board was the absolute last thing that he'd ever condone.

"Margaret Parsons?"

She gave the dead woman a few more seconds to reply, before scrolling down until she saw another female name.

"Carolina Heinz," she continued. "1890 to 1905. Are you in this room with me now?"

Although she was starting to feel as if she was on a hiding to nothing, she figured that she was already more than halfway through the process. She had no backup plan, no idea what to do if this particular approach failed, but she was keeping an eye on the various devices so that she'd notice immediately if any of them began to react. In the back of her mind she was starting to wonder whether she might be wasting her time, but she simply tried to focus on the fact that she was only at the very beginning of her ghost-hunting career – and that sooner or later she was going to hit upon something that actually worked.

"Carolina Heinz," she said again, "I just want to talk to you. I think you tried to contact me earlier, but I was too shocked to know how to respond. This time..."

Her voice trailed off, and after a few seconds she looked at her phone again. Scrolling further down, she finally found another name.

"Katrina Mulligan," she whispered.

She waited.

Silence.

"Katrina Mulligan," she went on, "you were the landlady here from 1935 to 1941 along with your husband Stephen, and then alone from 1941 to 1950. That's quite a long time. Certainly long enough for you to become intimately connected to this building. Are you the one who's haunting this place?"

Her words hung in the air for several seconds, but still there was no sign of any kind of response.

"Katrina Mulligan," she said yet again, with her finger still resting on the planchette. "Are you here with me now?"

***

"Is this actually going anywhere?" Derek asked with a sigh, standing in the front room up on the pub's first floor. "Don't get me wrong, I'm not doubting you. It's just that I'm not someone who usually goes around worrying about ghosts and stuff like that, and I can't help wondering whether we're just wasting our time."

"You might be right," Jonathan told him, "but don't you want to know for sure?"

"Mate, I just want an easy life," Derek admitted. "Unfortunately I'm not gonna get that unless my wife agrees to move back in. There's only so much that lazy lummox of a daughter can be expected to do." He glanced out toward the landing for a moment. "You got any kids?"

"A daughter," Jonathan replied. "And a young girl we're looking after as well."

"How old?"

"Thirteen and eleven."

"Oh, so you're just about to enter the years of maximum fun," Derek said with a faint smile. "I don't envy you. Don't get me wrong, Jane's a good girl, but all teenagers cause trouble in one way or another."

"Alicia's got her head screwed on straight," Jonathan replied, "and Rose... well, Rose is a little special, but she hasn't really been causing too much trouble so far."

"Just wait and see," Derek said, before craning his neck as he once again looked toward the landing. "Jane? Where are you? You were supposed to mop the floor in here but it doesn't like very mopped to me! I hope you don't think you can leave before you've finished all your chores!"

"My wife and I want to kind of... stake out the bar and the cellar tonight," Jonathan explained. "That might sound a little dramatic, but it's really the only way to determine once and for all whether there's anything down there. For reasons that we've never been able to determine, ghostly apparitions seem more inclined to make themselves known at night."

"So you're just going to sit up and wait to see if anything happens?"

"We have certain machines that we hope might give us an advantage."

"You do what you like," Derek replied. "I'll be up on the top floor, fast asleep and dreaming about all the things that might go wrong when we open for the first time in a few days from now. Just do me a favor, yeah? Don't come waking me up unless something really important happens. Spurs are playing and I usually need a good few drinks to get me through that."

He looked toward the door again.

"Jane?" he shouted. "You'd better still be here! If you've buggered off with your mates again, you're gonna be in so much trouble when you get back!"

"Do you think she's left?" Jonathan asked.

"I don't know what to think," he replied with a heavy sigh. "That's the thing about fathers and daughters. As they get older, girls start hiding things from you. Jane and I used to be so close when she was a little girl but now it's like she sees me as the enemy. You've got all that to come, of course. I must be -"

Before he could finish, he furrowed his brow as he continued to look toward the open doorway.

"Do you hear that?" he asked cautiously.

"Hear what?" Jonathan replied, before realizing that he could just about pick up the sound of several irregular bumps. "Where's it coming from?"

Stepping past him, Derek headed out onto the landing before stopping for a moment to look around. The sound was a little clearer now, although he still couldn't work out quite where it was coming from. Finally he walked over to the nearest door and looked into the living room, but there was still no sign of anyone. As the sound continued, he turned and looked over his shoulder just as Jonathan emerged from the kitchen.

"It seems to be coming from everyone at once," Jonathan pointed out, clearly puzzled. "I've never heard anything quite like it."

"This place is gonna be the bloomin' death of me," Derek said wearily. "The brewery reckon they only just fixed the boiler, but if it's already threatening to die again I swear I -"

Suddenly a framed photo flew from the opposite wall, slamming into the door next to Jonathan before falling down onto the floor. Glass was already falling from the frame.

"What the hell caused that?" Derek asked, hurrying to the window and looking out. "It's not an earthquake, is it? I never heard of an earthquake hitting Norfolk before, but you never know."

Stepping over to the broken picture, Jonathan picked it up and turned it around. The faded old photo inside showed a woman and a man standing in what appeared to be the bar downstairs, and some scrawled text at the bottom offered a pair of names.

"Stephen and Katrina Mulligan," he whispered, reading them out loud. "Are these former landlords of the place?"

"Probably," Derek told him. "There are pictures like that dotted all around, but to be honest with you I was thinking of taking most of them down. They're pretty creepy, and my wife wasn't too worried about the place until she started looking at the photo of the boy with the ball. That's when all the trouble really started."

"I should show this to my wife," Jonathan told him. "She might -"

In that moment a scream rang out from upstairs. Derek immediately began to hurry up the next set of stairs, and Jonathan followed him up to the pub's top floor. They could both hear a bumping sound coming from one of the bedrooms, and they hurried through just in time to see that Jane was hiding in the corner with her hands held up high to cover her face.

"Get her away from me!" she sobbed. "Don't let her touch me!"

"What are you talking about?" Derek asked, stepping over to her and reaching out to help her up, only for her to pull back further into the corner. "Jane, have you lost your mind? What's wrong with you?"

"There was a woman in here," she whimpered as tears streamed down her face. "She was right in front of me and she reached out. She tried to touch me. Dad, what the hell kind of place have you brought us all to?"

CHAPTER NINE

"ARE YOU KIDDING ME, Derek?" Elizabeth snapped, standing in the street outside the pub while glaring red-faced at her husband. "It's not going to magically just be fine! This place is haunted!"

"Lizzie -"

"And we're not setting foot in it again until it's been cleared out," she continued, stepping back and grabbing her daughter's hand. "Jane, you're coming with me and you're not working for your father again until this pub is declared safe!"

"It was just a misunderstanding!" Derek protested. "Come off it, when all's said and done do you seriously think there's a ghost in the pub? Hand on heart, Lizzie, you're a sensible woman. You can't actually think that there's something in there!"

"Oh, I believe it alright," she replied, "and I

can't believe that you haven't noticed a bloody thing! You've always been a bit of an insensitive old duffer, Derek Handley, but how can you have your eyes closed so much? When you brought those people in to check it out, I thought maybe you were finally coming round to reality but apparently you're just as stubborn as ever!"

"I brought them in to prove that there *isn't* anything here," he protested. "Why can't anyone else see that this ghost malarkey's just a load of nonsense? Lizzie, the pub's opening on Thursday! You can't -"

***

"- expect me to run the place single-handed. I need you. I need both of you. This whole thing doesn't work if it's just me doing everything!"

Sitting inside the gloomy bar area, Rebecca and Jonathan continued to listen to the argument outside. Ever since Elizabeth Handley's arrival a short while earlier, the shouting match had been getting louder and louder while Jane Handley had been lingering behind her mother with tears gathering in her eyes. Rebecca, meanwhile, was peering out through the window while Jonathan tried to keep busy by admiring the various beer pumps.

"Well," he said finally, breaking the silence,

"this is going well, isn't it?"

"That girl looks terrified," Rebecca pointed out.

"Oh, I'm sure she is," her husband murmured. "The thought of having to do some actual work must be positively horrifying."

Rebecca turned to him.

"I'm joking," he told her. "Sort of. Listen, I'm not sure that we should stick around much longer."

"Are you crazy?" she asked. "There's something here!"

"There might well be," he replied, "but we only seem to be making it worse."

"There's a ghostly entity in the pub's cellar," she reminded him. "This situation is ripe for investigation."

"Have any of your home-brewed devices actually picked up on anything?"

"No, but -"

"So maybe we've run into things a little too eagerly," he went on. "I was worried about this from the start. We should stand back and avoid getting so... emotional."

"You're referring to me," she replied, bristling slightly. "You're talking about the Alexander thing."

"I didn't use those words."

"But that's what you're thinking," she

continued, before pausing for a moment. "And I get it. The whole thing seems absurd, but I *swear* I heard her use his name. How is that possible unless she somehow..."

Her voice trailed off.

"I can't even begin to explain it," she added, "but it happened. I need to know how, and why."

"This was always supposed to be purely a scientific research project," he countered. "When our own emotional lives get drawn into that, we're no longer able to examine the evidence rationally. The moment you thought you heard Alexander's name mentioned, we should have immediately packed up and left."

"Well, it's too late for that now," she said as Elizabeth Handley raised her voice again outside. "You can't abandon an experiment halfway through, just because you don't like the way the results are going. Jonathan, you know that there's something here so -"

Before she could finish, the pub's front door swung open and Derek stepped through. Sighing, he let the door swing shut before standing for a moment in the gloom as footsteps stormed away outside. When he turned to Rebecca, the hangdog energy was impossible to miss.

"Jane, come back!" Elizabeth yelled in the street. "Young lady, don't you walk away from me!"

"I think I should cancel Thursday," Derek

said wearily.

"Why?" she asked.

"Because my wife's not going to help," he continued, "and there's no way I can launch the pub when it's just me. First impressions are crucial in this business and if I screw up the opening night, I might lose half my potential regulars on the spot."

"Then canceling might be a good idea," Jonathan suggested. "If -"

"No way," Rebecca said, making her way over to the bar to join them. "Give us one night, Mr. Handley. Give us tonight and I'm confident we can make some real progress. Your wife's right to be worried, there *is* a supernatural presence in your cellar but that doesn't mean it has to cause havoc. My husband and I are experienced when it comes to getting rid of such things."

"We are?" Jonathan whispered.

"We are," she said firmly, keeping her eyes fixed on Derek. "We've done it three times already now. Give or take. Please, we're not asking for a penny from you, Mr. Handley, we just want the chance to investigate a little further. Let us stay overnight and I'm confident that we'll be able to get to the bottom of it all."

"I don't know," Derek said, shaking his head. "This isn't quite what I signed up for."

"But it's what *we* signed up for," she reminded him. "If we can figure out who's haunting your cellar and why, we might be able to get rid of her. And then your pub will be able to open on Thursday and I'm sure it'll be a huge success."

"I'm confused," he replied. "I thought the ghost was a little boy with a ball, but now you're going on about a woman."

"We'll figure that out too," Rebecca said, before turning to her husband. "Won't we?"

"Sure," Jonathan said, although he didn't sound particularly confident. "Why not? I guess it's worth a shot."

"I suppose it won't hurt to give you a chance," Derek admitted. "Are you going to need me for any of this, or can I disappear upstairs and drown my sorrows for the rest of the evening? Spurs are playing and I'm hoping I can watch that and it might take my mind off everything that's going wrong with the world. You never know, they might actually manage to score a goal for once."

"Watch the football and try to forget about all of this," Jonathan said cautiously. "We'll do our best down here."

"We'll do more than that," Rebecca added. "We guarantee that by morning, your property will have been freed from whatever ghostly entity might be haunting it."

"We do?" Jonathan said, furrowing his brow as he turned to her.

"We do," she said firmly.

"I suppose I should be grateful," Derek said as he made his way behind the bar and grabbed a bottle of beer from the shelf. "Listen, I'm going to leave you alone to... work your magic. If you need anything, you know where to find me. Just don't go opening up any portals to Hell or anything like that. I've seen movies, I know how these things usually work out. If rabid giant monster dogs start crashing through the pub, my insurance might not extend to exorcisms or whatever else goes on here. I wouldn't be agreeing to this if I wasn't already at the end of my tether."

Heading to the hallway, he began to make his way up the stairs.

"And if I look out the window and see a giant marshmallow man," he added, "then I'll know that things are *definitely* going wrong."

"He doesn't believe we can do this," Rebecca said after a moment.

"Geez, I wonder why," Jonathan replied. "Might it be because we so obviously are in massively over our heads?"

"The ghost in the cellar touched me," she said, turning to him. "She literally reached out and touched me. And she whispered Alexander's name. And apparently she also touched Jane Handley. That means she *wants* to make contact, and she's hoping that we can give her something. Don't you get it, Jonathan? This ghost isn't hiding away in the shadows. I think she's doing her best to talk to us and to let us know how we can help her."

"We're not doing a very good job, then, are we?"

"There's..."

She hesitated for a few seconds, before checking her watch.

"There's one more... thing... that I think might be really useful here," she added. "Unfortunately I left it at home, but I can drive like the clappers and bring it back here before midnight. Would you be okay here alone for a few hours?"

"I'm not sure that another machine is going to be much help," he told her. "Why don't we focus on -"

"Trust me, this one will work," she said firmly, already grabbing her coat from the bench. She gave him a quick peck on the cheek as she hurried past. "We need to pull out all the stops, Jonathan. Hold the fort and I'll be back before you know it."

CHAPTER TEN

"HOLD THE FORT AND I'll be back before you know it," Jonathan muttered under his breath around an hour later, not sounding particularly impressed as he shone his flashlight around the cellar once more. "Sure, Rebecca. I'll hold the fort. And then you can show up with one of your clapped-out little devices that'll achieve absolutely nothing."

As much as he was trying to drum up some enthusiasm, in truth he really wasn't sure exactly what Rebecca expected him to do. He'd spent some time up in the bar trying to brainstorm a few ideas but in truth he felt somewhat at a loss. He didn't doubt for one second that there was *something* in the pub, but he felt sure that he and his wife couldn't simply storm into the place and expect to solve the mystery so quickly. The ghostly presence had most likely been present for the duration of many landlords' stints in the pub and evidently none of them had ever nabbed definitive proof.

How were he and Rebecca expected to do any better?

Finally, figuring that he was wasting his time, he turned to go back up the stairs. As he did so, however, he stopped suddenly as he realized that he could just about hear the faintest scraping sound coming from somewhere nearby. He looked back across the room and saw the barrels at the far end, but the scraping sound persisted and slowly he began to suspect that it was coming from one spot in particular.

Looking down at the cracked floor, he couldn't help but feel that something was scraping against the underside of the concrete.

Stepping forward, he shone the flashlight's beam at one of the larger cracks. He could see moisture glistening on the edges and he was fairly sure that the foundations of the pub were in a completely ruinous condition. Even breathing in the rather damp air of the basement felt dangerous, and a moment later he felt a section of concrete shifting slightly beneath his right foot as if the entire floor was in danger of sinking into some kind of vast swampy mess. Although he was far from an expert on the structural integrity of centuries-old buildings, he had to admit that he was glad he wasn't on the hook for any repair work that might need doing.

And as he stopped at the edge of the larger crack he realized that the scratching sound still hadn't stopped.

Crouching down, he shone the beam directly into the crack, although he found that he could only see some kind of dark muddy substance down in the gap. He tried angling the beam a few different ways, but after a moment he stopped and instead listened as the scratching persisted. After a few seconds he reached into his pocket and took out a pen, and then he carefully inserted one end into the crack and scratched the end against the concrete.

The two sounds were almost identical.

"What are you?" he whispered. "What caused all of this?"

He hesitated, but a moment later he heard a knocking sound coming from upstairs. He looked up and listened, and a few seconds later he heard the same thing again. This time he was certain that he knew exactly what was happening: someone was knocking on the pub's front door.

***

Once he'd ascertained from the sound of a chanting football crowd that Derek was busy upstairs, Jonathan made his way to the front door and pulled the bolt aside, before pulling it open and finding that a young man was standing outside.

"Are you him?" the man asked, sounding slightly breathless.

"I'm... someone," he admitted cautiously.

"Are you the guy who showed up to talk to Jessie earlier?"

"I am, but -"

"You don't want to listen to her," the guy continued. "I was with her when it all happened and I'm telling you right now, something seriously strange happened to her down there."

"Okay, calm down," Jonathan replied, before stepping aside. "Come in for a moment."

"My name's Taylor," the guy said as he stepped into the pub. Every single aspect of his body language was screaming discomfort and after a moment he looked down at the wooden floorboards as if he expected them to break apart and swallow him up. "This place is wrong. Seriously wrong. It should've been knocked down years ago."

"I imagine the trustees of the conservation area would have a thing or two to say about that," Jonathan suggested as he shut the door. "What -"

"Are you some kind of ghost researcher?"

"That's one way of putting it," Jonathan told him. "Listen, Jessie told me that she encountered a ghostly woman down in the cellar. She told me she was terrified, and her mother confirmed that she hasn't been quite the same again."

"But has she told you what the ghost said to her?"

"No, she didn't mention that," he replied, confused by this latest revelation.

"I heard her yelling," Taylor continued. "At first she was shouting for someone to leave her alone, but then it changed. After a minute or two, she kept saying over and over again that it wasn't true."

"That *what* wasn't true?"

"I don't know, but then she started shouting that she couldn't give her what she wanted."

"Her?"

"The ghost! Isn't it obvious?"

"I'm not sure that anything's obvious here," Jonathan admitted, taking a moment to scratch the back of his head.

"Later, after she was brought up, she denied it all," Taylor explained. "She flat out told me that I imagined it, but I know what I heard. Jessie kept on yelling that she had nothing to give her and that she couldn't help. I couldn't make out any other voices down there, but Jessie was definitely hearing something and it was like she was having a conversation with that... thing."

"A conversation about *what*, exactly?"

"If I knew, I'd have told you already," Taylor

said, sounding now as if he was fast running out of patience. "Listen, she's my friend, okay? Maybe even more than that. We get on really well, but ever since that night she hasn't been herself. She's been out of it and really distant, and just generally not herself."

"I got that impression from her mother."

"And she goes out alone at night," Taylor continued. "I don't know where and I don't know why, all I know is that she goes off and she won't tell anyone why. Man, it's really freaky and I hate to admit it, but something's seriously wrong with her. It's like she's looking for something."

"For what?"

"I don't know!" he hissed. "I want to help her but I don't know how!"

"It sounds like she went through quite an ordeal here," Jonathan reminded him. "What you're describing could quite possibly be nothing more than symptoms of P.T.S.D. and that means she needs to get qualified help from a professional. There's really nothing that a layman can do."

"What's a layman?"

"I get it, you're concerned about your friend," he continued, "but the best thing you can do for her is just try to encourage her to seek out professional treatment. I can dig out the names of a few people I recommend, but ultimately no-one can force her to go to them. It has to be -"

Before he could finish, they both heard a jeering roar coming from high up in the pub.

"I think Spurs have scored," Jonathan suggested. "Or possibly been scored against. It's kind of hard to tell the difference. Listen, thank you for taking the time to come and talk to me, it's obvious that you're a good friend to Jessie. As for the next step, I think it might be best if you -"

"Do you know about Katrina Mulligan?"

"Who?"

"She used to run this pub years ago," Taylor explained. "Before I was born. After everything that happened to Jessie I started to do some research and I found out a lot about all the people who used to have the place. And I can't be sure, but I kind of zeroed in on Katrina Mulligan as maybe being the ghost that's here."

"That's... a new name to me," Jonathan admitted. "I think. I'm not sure, I've heard a few names mentioned in the potted histories of the place. Listen, if -"

"Can I show you something?" Taylor asked. "It's next to another pub in town, but it's only down the street and I swear it'll only take a few minutes. It's about Katrina Mulligan and I think it might explain some of what's going on here at The Saracen's Head."

"I'm not sure I should leave," Jonathan said cautiously. "I'm waiting for my wife to get back with some kind of new machine or... some device she's cooked up."

"Please," Taylor continued, and the desperation in his voice was impossible to miss now. "Jessie's my best friend in the whole world and I'm worried that something really bad might be happening to her. You might be the only person who can save her. Can't you just come and look at what I found?"

CHAPTER ELEVEN

"KATRINA MULLIGAN," JONATHAN READ out loud as he stood in the cemetery, aiming his flashlight at a grave near an old oak tree. "1908 to 1950."

"That's her," Taylor explained. "That's her grave."

"Yes, I get that, but -"

"And her husband's grave too."

"Yes, I see that," Jonathan continued, looking once more at the name inscribed above Katrina's. "Stephen Mulligan, 1888 to 1941. They both died a long time ago. It's very sad, but people have to die eventually. I don't see what -"

"They had a baby."

Jonathan turned to him as drunk voices cried out from a nearby pub that was filled to the rafters while a band played inside.

"I found out about it during my research," Taylor went on. "They had a baby but it died in the early 1940s, just after Stephen died. I think it died while it was being born. I tried to find out some more details, but I couldn't be sure. Anyway, from what I can tell, Stephen Mulligan died and then a few months later his only child died while it was coming out into the world. That would have left Katrina all alone."

"Again, it's tragic but I doubt it's that unusual. Unfortunately, children die sometimes. That's just how the world works."

He felt a shiver run through his bones as those words left his lips. He knew he sounded harsh and uncaring, but he'd had to adopt that sentiment carefully over the years in order to avoid thinking too much about the son he'd lost. When Rebecca had almost fallen apart following the miscarriage, he'd found himself in the role of supportive husband and he'd been forced to deal with his grief as quickly and as discretely as possible. Sometimes he wondered if there might have been a better way to come to terms with what had happened, but he regularly reminded himself that at least he'd made it out the other side without breaking.

"But the kid's not buried here," Taylor pointed out.

"Hmm?" Jonathan replied as the band in the

pub launched into a particularly raucous new song.

"The kid," Taylor said, pointing at the grave. "Why isn't the kid on the stone?"

"There could be a number of reasons for that," Jonathan pointed out. "Believe it or not, there was a time not that long ago when newborn infants often weren't named for the first six months or so of their lives. Child mortality was so poor that often families... well, I suppose they didn't want to get too attached in case the worst happened."

"That's not all," Taylor told him. "After her husband died, Katrina Mulligan apparently went into deep mourning. She kept the pub running, but only just. And it's said that sometimes at night... she used to get up to strange things."

"Such as?"

"There were whispers that she was into witchcraft."

"People have been using allegations of witchcraft to demonize women for thousands of years," Jonathan replied. "Trust me, I could point you to hundreds of papers on the subject."

"Yeah, but what if this time it was true?" Taylor asked. "What if she was up to something weird?"

"Do you have any proof?"

"People claimed -"

"Apart from gossip and allegations," Jonathan added, before pausing for a moment in the hope that the younger man might start to understand the futility of his argument. "I didn't think so. Even in the 1940s, I'm sure the lot of a lonely widow in life wasn't particularly great. Poor Katrina was probably dogged by whispered accusations as she tried to keep her pub going. I'm amazed she stuck at it until she died, but let's be honest here. She probably had no other options."

"Ever since those days," Taylor replied, "people have talked about strange things happening in that pub. Every single landlord had been driven out by the ghost."

"And now you're adding hyperbole to the whole thing," Jonathan observed, struggling to contain a sense of amusement. "You need to calm down a little, Taylor. I appreciate that you're trying to work out how to help your friend, but joining a witch-hunt almost a century after the fact won't achieve anything. Apart from confirming a few depressing theories of my own, that is. Even if she'd lived and died today, I'm sure Katrina Mulligan would still have faced plenty of gossip. Some things never change."

***

A couple of minutes later, as he led Taylor back out of the cemetery, Jonathan wondered whether there were any further words of wisdom he needed to offer the young man. And then, before he had a chance to conjure up some great philosophical point, he heard a familiar voice somewhere nearby.

"Mum, please, can we just go back to Aunt Vic's?"

Turning, he was shocked to see Jane Handley standing nearby, pulling on her mother's arm. For her part, Elizabeth Handley had sat – or possibly partially collapsed – on the front step of a pub named The Jolly Gardener. The band was still rollicking through their set inside, but Elizabeth Handley was clearly worse for wear and after a moment she leaned against the door's jamb even as her daughter pulled again on her arm.

"Mum, I'm serious," Jane continued, sounding as if she was close to tears now. "Do we really have to do this every night?"

"Go home," Elizabeth murmured, seemingly on the verge of passing out. "No-one's forcing you to be here."

"I can't leave you like this!" Jane snapped.

"I'll find my way back," Elizabeth said as she began to close her eyes. "Pick me up a kebab on your way back, yeah? Just leave it on the living room table and I'll..."

Her voice trailed off as she began to fall asleep.

"Is everything okay here?" Jonathan asked cautiously.

"Does it look okay?" Jane replied, letting go of her mother's arm. "She's like this every night. I can't remember the last time she just spent an evening at home."

"Has this started since the trouble with the pub?"

"It's been going on for years," she said with a heavy sigh. "Meanwhile Dad just watches the football. Or the darts. Or the rugby. Or anything to distract himself from the fact that Mum's an alcoholic. Not that he's much better, sitting up there night after night with an endless supply of beer. I can't believe he convinced another brewery to let him take over a pub, not after we got forced out of the last one, but I suppose they're pretty desperate. You know what they call Dad round here, don't you?"

"Surprise me."

"The Pub-Destroyer," she continued. "I heard some people suggesting once that breweries just move him into pubs for six months so they can prove that the places aren't viable businesses, and then they can sell them to developers. To be honest, I wouldn't even be surprised if that's true."

Looking past Jonathan, she saw Taylor lingering a little further back.

"What are *you* doing here?" she snarled.

"Nothing," he said softly.

"I don't care," she continued, holding her

hands up as she took a step back. "Let her pass out on the step for all I care. She usually manages to crawl back home at some point, but I don't even mind if she doesn't this time. I'm going to find someone else to hang out with."

Turning, she began to storm away.

"Jane?" Jonathan called out. "Where are you going?"

"Probably to some guy's house," Taylor suggested. "Everyone knows she's gone off the rails, and in a town like Ladburton, people always talk." He looked down at Elizabeth as she started snoring. "And she's no better," he added derisively. "The Handleys have had a reputation in this part of the county for years. It's a shame, Jane used to be this really cool girl, but lately it's like something changed and she completely snapped. In fact, tonight's the first time I've seen her out when she's not even more hammered than her mum. I guess she couldn't get anyone to buy her some alcohol, but she'll find a house party somewhere and there'll be people who don't mind offering her some vodka."

"I had no idea that they were such a dysfunctional family," Jonathan said, checking his phone but seeing that there was still no word from his wife. "We can't just leave her here, though. Do you know where her sister lives?"

"Just round the corner," Taylor told him, "but... I don't mean to be rude, but she's not exactly on the small side. How are we supposed to get her home?"

"It'll have to be brute strength, I'm afraid," Jonathan replied. "Come on, you take one side and I'll take the other. Then we can try to walk her back to her sister's place." Somewhere in the distance, as the band continued to play, a bottle smashed loudly. "Welcome to the joys of a night out in suburban England."

CHAPTER TWELVE

THE FRONT DOOR OF The Saracen's Head stuck a little as Jonathan pushed, but finally he was able to get it open. Stepping back inside, he looked around the empty bar and felt for a moment as if the place seemed particularly dank and desolate. As he pushed the door shut and slid the bolt across, he couldn't shake the sense that the pub had already died and that any resuscitation attempts were doomed to failure.

Wandering to the bar, he pulled his phone out and saw that there was still no word from Rebecca. The time would soon be 10pm and he'd hoped that she might be back already, and part of him was quite looking forward to telling her about his adventure getting Elizabeth Handley back to her sister's house.

Looking down, he saw that there were still a few flecks of the woman's vomit on his left shoe.

"These people can't run a pub," he murmured as he heard music rumbling upstairs, no doubt from the television as Derek continued his post-football viewing. "They can't even manage their own -"

Before he could finish, he heard a loud bumping sound coming from somewhere below. He looked down again, this time at the floorboards beneath his feet, and he couldn't help but think of the pitch-black cellar far below. As much as he hated the idea of going back down there, he quickly told himself that there was no need to be scared, that he'd be fine just so long as he followed a strictly scientific approach. Sure, he could wait for Rebecca to return with whatever device she'd come up with now, but part of him liked the idea that he might be able to surprise her with a few positive developments of his own.

"You're not the only one who can investigate a haunting alone," he said, trying to give himself a little extra confidence. "I'll be fine."

He hesitated.

"As long as no ghostly deer jump off the walls and break my ribs."

***

As soon as he'd pulled the cord and the light in the cellar had switched on, he felt a little foolish for ever having been scared.

Looking across the cellar, he realized that he'd never seen such a banal place in his life. At least Marlstone Hall and Lotham Lodge had been grand and somewhat atmospheric locations. The cellar of The Saracen's Head, on the other hand, was a damp and cramped little space with a cracked floor and a distinctly musty smell. Sure, the place was fairly old, but any sense of history was ruined by the barrels of beer on the far side of the room and by the rather modern pipes running up to the bar above. All things considered, he had to admit that this particular space was about as scary as a motorway service station.

And yet...

And yet, as he stood at the foot of the staircase, he began to wonder whether this banality might in fact be the whole point. Wasn't he in danger of falling victim to a somewhat cliched view of ghosts? After all, there was no reason why a ghost should only haunt some gothic old house out in the middle of nowhere. In fact, the more he thought about it, the more he realized that ghosts should in theory be just as likely to haunt more mundane locations. After all, if the spirit of some deceased soul made the effort to come back, wouldn't they choose to haunt a place that mattered to them? Based on that logic, a brooding old country mansion was no more or less likely to be haunted than a motel or a supermarket or a corner shop.

Or the basement of a little pub in a nondescript and slightly dull town.

Stepping out across the cracked floor, he told himself that he had to stay focused. One of the concrete sections shifted slightly beneath his feet, and as he reached the middle of the room he was already having to remind himself once again that there might well be a ghost around. He turned and looked over his shoulder and saw the pile of boxes and bags his wife had left behind earlier, and he began to think back to the gravestone he'd seen earlier in the cemetery.

"Katrina Mulligan?" he said out loud, hoping to poke any ghostly presence a little. "Are you here?"

He waited, but he heard no sign of any answer.

"Katrina Mulligan," he continued, "if you're here, then you should know that I saw your grave earlier tonight. It's not far from here, actually. You're buried with your husband, although there's no mention on the stone of any child. But I heard a rumor that you had a child once, even if..."

His voice trailed off for a few seconds.

"Even if it didn't work out too well," he

added.

Standing in silence, he already felt like a fool. In fact, sometimes he wondered whether he'd been acting out of character ever since the events at Marlstone Hall three years earlier. Sure, he always told Rebecca that he was fully onboard with the whole ghost-hunting malarkey, but there were moments – quiet, private moments that usually settled in his soul like late-night snow – in which he found himself questioning the whole endeavor. Now, as he listened out for some kind of ghostly whisper but heard only a faint humming sound coming from some kind of chiller system hooked up to the beer barrels, he found himself experiencing another moment of doubt. What if he was wasting valuable time and ignoring more important research?

He already knew that some of his colleagues were laughing at him behind his back, and that he was risking a reputation that he'd carefully built up over many years. What if -

Suddenly, out of the corner of his eye, he spotted something moving past a nearby archway. He turned, but in that moment the solitary bulb flickered and died, plunging the cellar into darkness.

"Who's there?" he called out, and he was shocked now by the hint of fear in his own voice. "If there's someone there, you need to identify yourself at once."

Reaching into his pocket, he pulled out his phone. After activating the flashlight app, he held it up but saw only the empty archway now. He tried to convince himself that he'd been wrong earlier, that he'd merely imagined the figure, yet deep down he knew that wasn't the case.

"I know you're here," he went on. "I saw you, so there's no point hiding. I don't have time for silly games so you're only wasting your energy."

Hearing no reply, he stepped over to the archway and looked through. He hated the idea that someone might be playing some kind of prank, and he was by no means convinced yet that the other presence had to be ghostly. In fact, he felt sure that any ghost most likely wouldn't go sneaking around, although he quickly reminded himself that he risked rushing into another set of assumptions.

Exactly how was a ghost *supposed* to act?

"My name is Jonathan Pearson," he continued, "and I'm here to conduct some research. If the ghost of Katrina Mulligan – or the ghost of anyone, in fact – is here, then I would very much like to make contact and learn a little about you."

Again he waited, but deep down he knew that any ghost was highly unlikely to simply step into view, introduce itself and ask what he wanted to know. For some reason that he hadn't yet figured out, ghosts seemed to be far more irrational figures that were focused on one particular aspect of their former lives. At Lotham Lodge, for example, the ghosts had seemingly been trapped in a cycle that saw them constantly repeating one of the worst moments of their shared existence, although they'd certainly been able to interact with the living. He figured that ghosts – if indeed they were real – were certainly worthy of further study, but that they weren't exact replicas of the people they'd been while they were alive.

Instead they were almost -

Suddenly he heard a heavy gasping sound coming from somewhere over his shoulder, as if someone had taken a huge gulp of air. Turning, he held the phone up again, and this time he had to admit that his heart was racing.

"Who's there?" he snapped, trying but failing to hide a sense of anger. "Listen, I'm not going to put up with this. I'm not going to be made fun of or..."

Before he could finish, however, he realized that something had changed. Still holding the phone, he was just about able to see across the cellar, and to his horror he was starting to pick out a sound that was rising above the hum of the beer-chilling equipment.

Somewhere nearby – somewhere in the cellar – a baby was crying.

CHAPTER THIRTEEN

STEPPING FORWARD, JONATHAN TRIED to work out exactly where the sound of the baby was coming from. At first, as he looked all around, the sound seemed to be hanging in the air and reaching out to him from every direction at once, and he figured that the acoustics of the cellar were probably playing havoc with his efforts to pinpoint a specific location.

After a few more seconds, however, he realized that the sound seemed to be coming from one of the other small rooms nearby.

Making his way over to another of the archways, he stopped and looked through. The crying sound seemed a little further away now, or perhaps more muffled, but there was no mistaking the fact that a baby was apparently crying somewhere in the cellar.

"Hello?" he said cautiously, before reminding himself that a baby wasn't about to offer any kind of response.

In that moment the sound seemed to fade a little. Wondering whether it had somehow moved into another room, Jonathan retraced his steps and walked over to another archway, and for a moment the sound became a little clearer. Somehow the child's cries seemed to be moving fairly quickly through the entire basement area of the pub, and sure enough after just a few more seconds the noise seemed to shift and withdraw again before finally coming to a somewhat abrupt end.

Although he waited for the sound to return, Jonathan began to realize that the crying child had apparently faded away to nothing. And then, a moment later, he heard a shuffling sound and he turned to see that he was no longer alone in the cellar.

Whereas a moment earlier there had been nobody else around, now he saw what appeared to be a woman wearing a pale old-fashioned dress, standing in the far corner with her back turned to him. Her sudden appearance was so incongruous yet so blunt that for a few seconds Jonathan couldn't quite believe his own eyes. He blinked a couple of times, convinced that the image was going to somehow dissipate, but gradually he began to realize that it seemed to be very real.

"Hello?" he said finally, worried about chasing the strange figure away. "Can you hear me?"

He waited, but the figure showed no sign that it was even aware of his presence. Although he couldn't see its face, he could tell that this was a woman; her long dark hair hung down against the back of her dress and he could see her thin, somewhat spindly hands on either side. She was slightly hunched, as if she was leaning slightly into the corner, but he assumed that for whatever reason she must have *chosen* to be visible in that moment.

Was this, he wondered, some first stab at communication?

"I don't know if you heard me earlier," he said, taking a step forward, "but... my name is Jonathan Pearson and I'm here to investigate this pub. Well, this cellar, really."

Again he waited, hoping for a response, and after a few seconds he dared to hold the phone up a little higher. He could certainly make the woman out a little better now, and he could see that her dress was indeed old and very frayed. Although he was far from an expert on such matters, he felt that this was certainly something that might have been worn by a pub landlady back in, say, the early to mid twentieth century.

"Are you Katrina Mulligan?" he continued.

"Is -"

Before he could finish, the figure turned its head slightly to the right, and the movement was accompanied by a faint crunching sound as if the bones in her neck hadn't shifted for a while.

He still couldn't see her face properly, but Jonathan at least knew now that the woman could hear him. Convinced that his next words were crucial and could make or break the entire investigation, he tried to work out how best to keep the contact going.

"I'm going to assume," he said after a few seconds, "that you *are* Katrina Mulligan. You lived here a long time ago, didn't you? If I'm right, you died... seventy-four years ago. Have you been down here ever since? That's a long old time to be wandering around in the cellar. Something pretty important must have been keeping you here."

He waited, but so far the woman hadn't reacted again. The only thing that had caught her attention seemed to be her name, so he decided to try a different approach.

"Your husband was Stephen," he reminded her. "Stephen Mulligan. He died in... 1941, wasn't it? So you spent the last nine years of your life alone here, running the pub by yourself. That must have been very challenging."

Watching her carefully, he wondered why she still hasn't fully turned to face him.

"And then there was the child," he added, deciding to try to dig a little deeper into her psyche. "You had a child, I believe, but he or she died in the womb. Something similar happened to my wife and myself a long time ago. I know how much it hurts and..."

As his voice trailed off, he saw that she was slowly raising her right hand. Extending a finger, she appeared to be pointing toward one of the larger cracks on the floor.

"I've seen those," he told her. "Were they here in your day too? To be honest, they look fairly new but I might be wrong. My wife would happily tell you that I'm often wrong about a lot of things."

Looking down at the cracks again, he tried to work out why the woman was pointing.

"I heard a child crying just now," he continued, turning to the woman again. "Not too clearly, but... enough to be sure that it was real. But it stopped quite suddenly and as far as I know there's really not supposed to be a baby on the premises, so I can't help wondering..."

Once again he waited, worried that at any moment he might say too much and scare the ghostly figure away.

"What it *your* child?" he asked. "I must confess, I'm a little sketchy when it comes to the details. Was your child still alive when it was born? I know this must be hard for you to even think about but -"

Suddenly the woman turned and glared at him, and he let out a shocked gasp as he saw the darkness in her eyes. In that moment any last lingering doubts drained away and he realized that he was indeed face-to-face with a ghost.

"Where is your child buried?" he continued, and he couldn't help looking at the crack in the ground again. "You didn't bury him here, did you? Or her. That wouldn't make a whole lot of sense, but then again, I know for a fact that grief can make people do crazy things."

Stepping over to the larger crack, he kept an eye on the woman while slowly kneeling down to get a closer look. He touched the crack's edge and felt the cold concrete, and then he slowly and slightly hesitantly began to dip his hand deeper until he felt something cold and wet and muddy in the depths.

"It's not much of a grave," he whispered, "but then again, this isn't much of a cemetery."

He looked up at the dead woman, who was watching him intently now. As he met her gaze once more, he couldn't help but notice that the temperature in the entire cellar seemed to have dropped significantly in a matter of just a few seconds.

"Is your child in here?" he asked. "No offense, but that seems like the kind of bat-shit insane thing that tends to make ghosts stick around. Is your child in here and now you want it moved to sacred ground? Is that what's going on?"

Although he knew that his theory sounded like the plot of some straight-to-TV horror movie, he couldn't help thinking that it made at least a sliver of sense. Yet as he inched his hand a little deeper into the gap, he found himself wondering how he or anyone could ever find the bones of a child if those bones had spent decades slowly sinking into the foundations beneath the pub. Sure, he might get lucky and chance upon the bones near the top, but it was just as likely – more so, perhaps – that those same bones would have gradually sunk to depths from which they might never be recovered.

"I don't know how to help you," he told the woman. "Is there any chance you could give me a little more of a clue here?"

As those words left his lips, he realized that he could just about hear the child crying again. Looking over his shoulder, he felt once more as if the sound was echoing all around him, as if it was coming from every part of the cellar at once. He looked first once way and then another, convinced that at any moment the source of the sound was going to crystallize, but a few seconds later silence returned.

"I don't get it," he muttered, before turning to the woman again. "I -"

In that moment he saw to his horror that she was right next to him. Before he had a chance to pull away, she grabbed him by the throat and hauled him up from the floor, slamming him into the wall with such force that the back of his head hit the bricks hard. As he passed out, the last thing he heard was the woman's anguished scream.

CHAPTER FOURTEEN

"JONATHAN?" REBECCA SAID, NUDGING her husband's shoulder again as he slowly began to wake up. "What are you doing on the floor? What happened to you?"

Staring up at her, Jonathan took a moment to pull his thoughts together before suddenly he remembered the ghostly figure screaming at him. Startled, he sat up so fast that he almost headbutted his wife – and they only avoided contact because she pulled away at the last second.

"Where is she?" he asked.

"Where's who?"

"The woman."

Stumbling to his feet, he felt a sharp pain on the back of his head as he looked around. A moment later he held his hand up and saw that it was still partially caked in some of the muddy gunk from the crack in the floor.

"Jonathan, what happened down here?" Rebecca asked. "When we got back I couldn't find you anywhere. I was about to wake Derek up when I figured you might be in the cellar and then..."

She looked him up and down as if she genuinely couldn't understand why he was in such a state.

"Mulligan," he stammered, finally turning to her. "Katrina Mulligan. That's the name of the ghost."

"How do you know?"

"I'll explain later," he continued, "but I'm absolutely certain. And whatever's going on here, it has something to do with the baby she lost all those years ago. I heard a baby crying down here, Rebecca." He looked at the crack in the concrete floor. "I think for some reason she buried her dead child here, and maybe now she regrets that and she wants him exhumed so that he can be buried properly. With her and her husband in the cemetery in town."

"That... sort of makes sense," Rebecca acknowledged, "but I don't quite get how we're supposed to help her. We can't go ripping up the basement just to look for a tiny set of bones."

"I know," he replied, "but that's what she wants. She probably isn't being rational about the whole thing."

"Did she say anything else?"

"She didn't really say anything at all. I sort of deduced it from a few things." He hesitated for a moment. "That's what these ghosts are, Rebecca. If you think about it, every ghost we've encountered has been a kind of... distillation of the one or two key aspects of the person's character. It's as if, in death, their soul gets pared down until all that's left is the most important part of them. And for Katrina Mulligan, that core element seems to have been her grief for her child, or her regret for what happened to him."

"And she understands the suffering of others," Rebecca suggested. "That must be how on some instinctual level she knew about Alexander."

"So what are we supposed to do next?" he asked, sounding a little desperate now. "Short of bringing in a team to rip up the floor down here, and risk causing the pub to collapse in the process, how are we ever going to help this dead woman?"

He waited for a reply, but already he could see that his wife was lost in thought.

"Wait a moment," he added. "You're back, that's great, but did you get the thing you left back at home?"

"Yes," she said cautiously, as if she was choosing her words with great care. "I got the... thing that I thought might help."

"So where is it?"

"It's upstairs."

"Then bring it down."

Again he waited, but he could tell that something was bothering her.

"What is it?" he asked finally. "What's this device you had to go all the way home to collect?"

***

"It smells funny in here," Rose said, standing in the bar upstairs and looking around. "It smells like... really old and really stale beer."

"I should have guessed," Jonathan muttered, turning to his wife. "You said *we*. You said when we got back."

"I didn't tell you my plan earlier," she replied, "because I wasn't sure that you'd approve. But the thing is, we've been wanting to test Rose's abilities for a while and I figured the best way to do that would probably be to bring her out into the field. So to speak."

"And peanuts," Rose added. "I can smell peanuts."

She paused before offering a broad smile.

"I'm RP6!"

"That was just a joke," Rebecca hissed, nudging her.

In response, Rose merely twitched her upper

lip for a moment.

"It's late," Jonathan pointed out. "I'm not sure -"

"I know it's not ideal," Rebecca continued, lowering her voice a little, "but you have to admit that it has a chance of working. All I'm suggesting is that we take Rose into the cellar and see what she's able to pick up. And don't worry about Alicia, she's safe and sound back at home with Mum."

"There's a dead spider on the counter," Rose said, furrowing her brow. "Or bar, whatever you call it. Wait, do spiders have ghosts? Does *everything* have ghosts? What about bacteria?"

"Let's try to stay focused," Rebecca told her. "Don't worry, Rose, we're not going to be here long. I'll be getting you home just as soon as you've... helped us out with a few things."

"I'd love to know what the agency would think about this," Jonathan said, checking his watch and seeing that the time was almost midnight. "When we took Rose in, they didn't specifically say that we couldn't get her out of bed in the middle of the night and drive her to a pub for a ghost hunt, but they probably thought that was implied."

"I know we're not going to win any awards for this," Rebecca told him, "but the situation's a little unusual."

Stepping over to Rose, she put a hand on the girl's shoulder.

"As I mentioned in the car," she continued, "we just want you to have a little look around in the cellar here and see if anything leaps out at you."

"Something's going to leap out at me?" Rose gasped.

"Not literally," Rebecca replied. "Sorry, that was a poor choice of words. The point is, there's no right or wrong answer and it's absolutely fine if you don't pick up on anything. It's just that in the past you've shown that you have a certain ability to understand these things, and we could really use your help at the moment. Think of it as an adventure."

"I don't know if I want to have an adventure," Rose admitted.

"It won't be a scary adventure," Rebecca said, before turning to Jonathan. "Will it?"

"Let's hope not," he murmured.

"Are you trying to talk to the ghost?" Rose asked.

"Do you sense something already?" Rebecca replied, looking down at her again.

Rose hesitated before looking around the bar for a moment.

"Maybe," she said softly.

"Is it a kind of presence?"

"I think there's something here," Rose continued, before nodding. "No, there's *definitely* something here. I can't see it and I can't hear it, but somehow I still know that it's here." Slowly she looked down at the floorboards. "It's everywhere. Can't you tell?"

"Not to the same extent that you can, apparently," Rebecca replied. "I'm really sorry that we're kind of using you like this, Rose, but I hope you know that we wouldn't do it if the situation wasn't an emergency. But I promise you that it's not going to be scary and that we won't let anything bad happen. It'll just take five minutes, all you have to do is come down into the cellar with us and tell us if you notice anything. Are you still okay with that?"

Rose thought for a moment, and then slowly she nodded.

"Why don't we get it over with, then?" Rebecca said, taking the girl's hand and starting to lead her through into the hallway. "Like I told you, it really doesn't have to take too long or -"

Stopping suddenly, she saw a shadowy figure standing in the hallway. For a fraction of a second she froze, terrified that the ghostly figure from the cellar might have emerged, but a moment later the figure stepped forward.

"What are you doing?" Jane asked.

"Hey," Rebecca said cautiously. "We just, uh..."

"We're ghost-hunting," Rose explained. "Do you want to join us?"

"No," Jane replied, shaking her head, "I

don't. I just came home to pick up some things. Are you guys going to be poking around down there all night?"

"Your dad wants us to get to the bottom of whatever's going on here," Rebecca reminded her.

"Whatever," Jane said, rolling her eyes as she turned and headed through to the kitchen at the rear of the pub. "You guys are crazy. You know that, right? You're just trying to make money by tugging on the fears of idiots."

"We don't charge for any of this," Rebecca called after her. "Jane? We actually spend our own money on a lot of it. Most of the time we're running at a loss!"

She waited for a reply, but a moment later the kitchen light flickered on and she heard the girl opening the fridge door.

"Are we going down *there*?" Rose asked, looking toward the open door that revealed the rickety stairs descending into the cellar. "It looks spooky." She paused, and then she smiled. "I like it."

CHAPTER FIFTEEN

"REMEMBER," REBECCA SAID AS she, Rose and Jonathan stood in the cellar with the light now working again. "There's no wrong answer and you won't be in trouble if you don't pick up on anything at all. We just want to see if you notice anything."

"It's cold," Rose said after a moment.

"Here," Rebecca replied, quickly removing her own coat and hanging it over the girl's shoulders. "That should help."

"It smells funny," Rose continued, scrunching her nose a little. "Like it's been wet for a long time."

She looked down at the cracks in the concrete.

"The smell's coming from down there," she explained. "I changed my mind. I don't think I like it down here very much at all. It's like -"

Suddenly she turned and looked at one of the archways, as if something in another part of the basement had caught her attention.

Rebecca waited for her to say something, before turning to her husband. He, in turn, could only shrug.

"She's here," Rose whispered.

"Who's here?" Rebecca asked.

"Katrina."

Again Rebecca looked at Jonathan, and this time he seemed far more interested in what Rose was saying.

"She's sad about her baby," Rose went on. "She thinks it's her fault that it died. She was sad about her husband already, and she thinks because she was sad she made her baby sad and... and that's why it died inside of her." She paused for a few more seconds. "She didn't want them to take it away, so she hid it, and she tried to find out if there was anything she could do to bring it back to life."

"Where exactly did she hide it?" Jonathan asked cautiously. "In... in here?"

Rose looked around for a moment before confidently pointing at one particular spot on the cracked floor.

"There?" Jonathan continued, before turning to Rebecca. "When I saw her... I think that's where she pointed."

"She tried and she tried," Rose explained. "And she tried and tried and tried, for days and nights. She had lots of ideas but... I don't think any of them worked, and she got more and more desperate. She was getting books from the library and trying to find things from local history, from anything." A single tear appeared in the girl's left eye and quickly began to run down her cheek. "It was horrible," she added softly. "She didn't know why it wasn't working. She was worried she was failing her baby again."

A flicker of recognition ran across Rebecca's features.

"And then she lost him," Rose continued. "She lost him in the mud under the floor and she couldn't find him again. She knows he's still down there and she knows she'll never be able to find him, but that doesn't stop her wanting to try. I think she's trapped here by that. She thinks that leaving would be like abandoning her baby and that idea would break her heart. So she stays here all alone, and sometimes she tries to find him again but mostly she just misses him and wishes she could make everything better."

"A tragic story," Jonathan pointed out. "But how are we supposed to help her if we literally can't do the one thing that she wants? Short of ripping the pub down and sifting through meters of mud beneath the concrete, how are we ever going to let her see that she can leave?"

"I think it has something to do with *how* she was trying to get her baby back," Rose said, furrowing her brow a little as she continued to stare at the concrete. "I think she did it in a way that means she's stuck here forever. Or at least, she thinks she is."

***

1941...

"It's fine," Katrina Mulligan sobbed, slowly kneeling on the cellar's smooth concrete floor as she cradled the fabric bundle in her arms. "My precious little darling, Mummy's here and everything... everything is going to be just fine."

Above, voices were calling out and laughing in the bar. Although the war had greatly changed the pub's operations, The Saracen's Head was just about managing to survive even if most customers only managed one or two pints during the evening. That was still enough to make the place lively, sometimes even when air raids were threatened, and this particular night was no exception. As Katrina carefully set the fabric bundle on the floor, the laughs coming from upstairs seemed almost to be mocking her predicament.

"Mrs. Mulligan?" a voice called out from

the top of the stairs. "If -"

"I told you to serve yourselves!" she snapped.

"But -"

"Don't come down here!" she continued, turning and glaring toward the staircase, where she saw a shadow cast by whoever was at the top. "I swear... serve yourselves and put the money on the bar."

She waited, but fortunately the interloper turned and walked away.

Looking back down at the bundle on the floor, Katrina realized to her horror that part of the cloth had come away, revealing a solitary and very small discolored hand. She quickly covered the hand up again before glancing around at the candles burning nearby, and then she picked up the latest tattered book she'd checked out of the library. The cover was sparse, but the spine revealed the title:

Rituals of the Home Counties: Superstitions and Paganism in Rural England

"One of these must have at least a shred of truth about it," she muttered as she flicked through the pages. "Eventually."

For the next few minutes, as more voices laughed and cheered above, Katrina studied the book intently. The author hadn't set out to offer lists of spells, of course, but he'd included enough information to allow any interested reader to cobble together their own versions. And as she turned to another page and read about spring fertility rituals from up north, she realized that she could perhaps apply some of those rituals to the task at hand.

"It's alright, my darling," she murmured. "Mother's going to find a way to give you everything you deserve. You never even had a chance to draw a single breath. Mother's going to change that."

She read the same few paragraphs several times before reaching over and grabbing the box of herbs she'd gathered earlier in the day. Setting some of them on top of the bundle, she also took out a knife and a few other items. All she knew in that moment was that she had to find some way to bring life to her dead child, and finally she took the knife and began to cut into her own palm. Wincing, she turned the hand over and let blood dribble down onto the herbs, with some of the precious red liquid splattering against the fabric itself and – she hoped – sinking deep enough to reach the dead child within.

"I pray to Frig," she said out loud, using the name of an old Anglo-Saxon goddess she'd found in the book, "that she might bless this child with the gift of life."

Glancing at the book again, she took a

moment to refamiliarise herself with the scant details of some old ritual.

"Please, Frig, look upon us and show mercy," she continued as tears began to fill her eyes. "Put right that which has gone so horribly wrong here."

She waited, but all she heard were more cheers coming from upstairs and all she saw was her own cooling blood staining the fabric bundle. Part of her wanted to try uttering the prayer again – and again, and again and again if that was what it took – yet deep down she already knew that this latest attempt had failed. Her dead child was relying on her to bring life to death, yet she felt as if she was once again proving herself to be a terrible mother. After all, she hadn't even been able to carry him to term in her body; now that he was out, she told herself over and over that she was proving herself to be a terrible mother in every possible respect.

"I just want my child," she whimpered as tears ran down her face. "He's all I have left. Why can't he and I be together?"

Sobbing heavily now, she leaned back against the wall as candles continued to burn. She'd said so many prayers to so many gods that now any prayer at all felt worthless. Deep down she was worried that her efforts were all going to be in vain, but she quickly told herself that she had to keep trying. Indeed, she knew that she was *never* going to give up, that if necessary she would spend the rest of her days trying every possible ritual that might bring her child to life. And if they all failed, then she was just going to have to invent some of her own.

"I'll never abandon you," she sobbed as the child's body remained on the floor, wrapped in various cloths and towels. "I'm your mother and I *will* find a way to save you."

CHAPTER SIXTEEN

"IT'S VICTORY," ERNEST TOWNSEND said four years later as he stood in the bar of The Saracen's Head and admired the pint of beer he'd just sampled. "That's what it tastes like. It tastes like ruddy victory."

Cheers erupted as the V.E. Day celebrations continued. All day the atmosphere in the pub had been filled with jubilation as customers had flocked out of their homes to celebrate the news that Germany had surrendered. Impromptu street parties had been set up across the country as people pooled their meager rations and tried to find a way to celebrate, and the mood in the town was one of indefatigable defiance. Many men from the area had died in the war and everyone knew that life was never going to be the same again, yet all the suffering – all the air raids and rationing – had eventually led to an outpouring of relief.

Over in the corner, a dozen men were crowding around an older fellow who'd managed to obtain a copy of a newspaper. Everyone was eagerly trying to find out as much as possible about what might happen next.

"We fought for it," Ernest continued, before looking over at the landlady. "Eh, Katty, old bird? There were those who said we should surrender and try to make peace, but we fought and now look at us."

Having barely heard those words, Katrina was merely staring into space as she tried to think of yet another spell variation that might help her plans. She'd been trying for years now to bring her dead son back to life, working for hours every night in the pub's cellar, yet the opposite had happened; rather than stirring and becoming a living child, the corpse had begun to rot away to nothing. Now, realizing that her sleeve had slipped up to expose the many scars on her arm, she quickly pushed the sleeve back down and told herself that she had to attend to business.

"I get it, you know," Ernest said as more cheers rang out in the street. "They're all celebrating, as well they might, but for some of us things are different. I know you lost your Stephen early on in the war, and nothing will ever bring back our loves ones who're gone. This can be a lonely old world."

"Mustn't complain," she replied, adopting the phrase she'd used so often during the war years. "There's them that's got it worse than us."

"Aye, that's true," Ernest acknowledged, nodding sagely. "Grumbling won't get anyone anywhere, either. Now we've got to rebuild, and that's not exactly going to be an easy process." He paused for a moment, watching Katrina's face as he saw that she seemed to be lost in her thoughts. "Are you going to be staying on here?" he asked. "I wouldn't ordinarily stick my nose in, only there's some around who heard you might be moving on."

"Moving on to *where*, exactly?" she asked. "I've nowhere else to go. I'll be behind this bar until my dying day, Ernie. I've got no choice."

"I suppose there are worse places to be," he murmured, before taking another sip of beer. "We've got it pretty good, out here in our little corner of England."

"There's too much work to do," Katrina told him as she glanced down at the wooden floorboards. "The war might be over, but that doesn't mean there'll be no more suffering. For some of us, at least."

***

Many hours later, once the pub had finally closed and the revelers had dispersed to continue their celebrations elsewhere, Katrina Mulligan sat once more on the floor of the cellar with candles burning all around.

In front of her, the bundle of fabric remained where it had remained for many years now. A long time had passed since Katrina had last dared to open the bundle and had looked at what was inside; she knew that the tiny body had rotted away and that there would be little left except bones, but she told herself that there was no need to force herself to look at that miserable sight. Instead she was still trying to find some miraculous combination of words and deeds that might snatch the child back from the jaws of death.

On this particular evening, however, she felt as if the last of her determination was on the verge of failing.

"I have prayed and prayed," she said out loud, shocked by the feebleness of her own voice, "to every god whose name I have found in any book, and they have all..."

Her voice trailed off as she stared at the bundle on the floor.

"They have all ignored me," she continued. "Every last one of them. Perhaps some of them did not hear, perhaps some of them were never real to begin with. But those that truly existed have ignored me and have not seen fit to come to my... to *our* aid. But I wonder..."

She hesitated again.

"I wonder whether there are any I have missed," she said, slowly closing the latest library book. "I wonder whether there are any whose names are too fearsome and too dreadful to be included in any book. Perhaps the ink itself would burn the page if their names were ever set down, so tonight..."

Wondering for a moment whether she should dare to go to the last extreme, she quickly reminded herself of her promise to her dead child.

"Tonight I pray to the overlooked gods," she whispered. "To the neglected gods. To the feared but forgotten gods. To *any* god from any tradition... any god that might show pity on me and on my poor lost child. If any god is out there in the darkness between the others, I pray that you might come to this place and show mercy to us. If you have the power to help us, we will do anything in return."

She waited.

She heard only silence.

"Anything," she added.

Again she waited, and after a few seconds her shoulders slipped and her back rounded. She knew the bitter, familiar taste of defeat, but she told herself that she would simply have to find some other way to get help. That, though, would be for another night, so she wearily got to her feet and began to trudge toward the staircase.

"It has been a long day," she murmured, "and -"

Suddenly she heard a loud cracking sound. Stopping at the foot of the steps, she hesitated for a moment as the sound continued. Slowly she turned, and to her shock she saw a single long crack slowly making its way across the cellar's concrete floor.

"What in the name of -"

Before she could finish, another crack appeared – and then another, forming a crude circle that seemed to be keeping the dead child at its center. In that moment, terrified that something might happen to her child, Katrina took a step forward and reached down to grab the bundle; at the last second, however, a chunk of the concrete floor rose up and tripped her, knocking her back down hard as all the candles instantly burned out and the entire cellar was plunged into darkness.

Too scared to move a muscle, Katrina remained on the floor and listened to a slow shuffling sound that was now filling the air.

"Is someone there?" she called out as the sound continued. "Who are you? What are you doing here?"

After a few seconds the sound faded away to nothing.

Leaning forward, Katrina reached out for

the bundle on the floor, but she found nothing at all. A moment later the cracking sound returned and she realized that the floor itself felt as if it was becoming unstable. Trying not to panic, she reached around in a desperate attempt to find her child's body, and then she reached back and found one of the candles. Pulling out a box of matches, she fumbled for a moment before managing to light one, which she used in turn to bring life once more to the candle. She then held the candle up and turned around, and she saw to her horror that the bundle of fabric had vanished from the floor.

"Where are you?" she stammered. "What -"

In that moment she spotted a piece of fabric hanging down in the air. She looked up, and then she let out a shocked gasp as she saw that the bundle was now somehow hovering above her; for a few seconds her scrambled brain was unable to process the image, until one piece of fabric fell away to reveal the collection of bones that were still somehow holding together. She had no idea how her son's body was floating in mid-air, but finally she began to reach out toward him, only to stop as soon as she heard another sound starting to fill the space.

Laughter.

Someone or something was letting out a low, rumbling laugh.

"Who are you?" Katrina stammered. "What do you want with us? Are you here to help us or -"

Suddenly the ground cracked open. Falling back, she landed hard on her elbow; the candle fell too but miraculously continued to burn until she grabbed it and tilted it up again. She saw that the floor had begun to tear itself apart, revealing the muddy ground beneath, and a moment later the unthinkable happened: her son's tattered body fell down and slammed into the mud with force, quickly sinking beneath the surface.

"No!" she shouted, crawling forward and reaching down, trying desperately to save him. "Stop! What are you doing?"

Pushing her hand deeper and deeper into the mud, she felt nothing but cold liquid. She tried over and over to find the bones, yet already she was terrified that he'd been taken from her forever.

"Bring him back!" she screamed as the laughter became louder all around her. "Please, don't do this! You have to bring him back to me!"

CHAPTER SEVENTEEN

"I DON'T KNOW ABOUT that, Mavis," Deirdre said as she and her friend pushed their prams along a narrow, winding street near the seafront. "People round these parts won't like that sort of thing. They'd be better off focusing on what's going on down the pit."

"No-one cares about any of that," Mavis replied forlornly. "Face it, our husbands and all those other men down there are seen as completely disposable." She took a drag on her cigarette. "They're barely one step above the pack animals."

Reaching down, Deirdre made a cursory effort to wave cigarette smoke away from her baby's face.

"Nothing was done after that last accident," Mavis continued. "Everyone knows there's no safety down there, not really. Peter Sandford died a year ago and no-one even talks about him much these days."

Reaching the steps outside a local pub, they both peered inside and listened to the sound of voices muttering away in the gloomy bar area.

"Do you want to pop in for a few minutes?" Mavis asked with a faint smile on her lips. "They'll be closing in half an hour or so anyway."

"I really shouldn't," Deirdre replied, even though she was clearly on the brink of falling for temptation. "What will people say?"

"It's just *The George*," Mavis pointed out. "It's hardly a den of iniquity. It's not like I'm trying to drag you into somewhere disreputable."

"I'd take that over *The Saracen's Head*," Deirdre said, before hesitating for a moment. "I don't want to take Baby in there, though. He's already got enough smoke in his lungs from the walk here."

"They'll both be alright out here for a little while," Mavis said, taking a few seconds to adjust the blankets in her child's pram before stepping around him and making her way into the pub. "You need to stop worrying so much. This town's too boring for anything bad to happen."

"Just wait for Mother," Deirdre said, leaning down and kissing her child before skipping up the steps and following her friend into the pub. "Wait for me, Mavis!" she called out. "I don't want you getting a head-start. And we can't leave the children out in the street for too long, or someone might start talking about us. The last thing I need is to have old Tilda telling everyone around town that I'm a bad mother."

As their voices merged with the general throng of conversation inside the pub, the two prams remained on the pavement outside. After a couple of minutes, however, a figure stepped out from around the corner and glanced in both directions before hurrying across and peering into the prams. A moment later, once she was sure that there was no-one around, the figure grabbed one of the prams and began to wheel it away along the street.

***

"It's such a miracle that I got you back," Katrina said, sitting on the pebbly beach with the baby resting on her lap. "I never gave up hope, not even once, but the wait..."

Staring down at the child, she watched as he giggled.

"You're so happy," she murmured, ignoring the voices calling out in the streets nearby. "You know Mummy would never let anything bad happen to you, don't you? We'll just gloss over the past few years and instead we'll focus on the bright future ahead of us. You know, your father would have been so proud of you. He's just -"

"Terry!"

Hearing footsteps racing across the pebbles, Katrina looked up just in time to see several men and women hurrying down the beach. Before she had a chance to react, one of the women grabbed the child from her arms and pulled him away.

"What are you doing?" Katrina stammered.

"You mad old shrew!" Mavis snarled, kissing the child several times before turning to glare at her. "What's wrong with you? We all know who you are, Katrina Mulligan, but none of us realized you were the type to go around snatching babies in broad daylight!"

"Snatching babies?" Katrina stammered, stumbling to her feet as a few other people joined the scene. "What are you talking about? Give my child back to me!"

"*Your* child?" Mavis spluttered. "You're not right in the head!"

"She hasn't been right in the head for years," Deirdre said slightly breathlessly. "Everyone knows it. When her husband died, something went wrong with her and it's never been fixed. That's one of the reasons I always tell my Douglas that he's not to set foot in her pub. And I'm not the only one who says that, either."

A murmur of agreement rumbled across the crowd.

"I don't know what you're talking about," Katrina said as tears began to fill her eyes. She reached again for the child, but again he was pulled away from her. "What's wrong with you all? Why are you being like this? I just want to be left alone with my darling boy."

"He's not your darling boy," Mavis sneered. "He's my little Terry, and he's coming home with me right now. I only left him outside for a few minutes while I was on some errands, and you swooped in and tried to steal him!"

"No," Katrina said, shaking her head, "you've got it all wrong. I was..."

As her voice trailed off, she realized that she'd left the pub in order to visit a few of the shops. She tried to convince herself that she'd had the baby with her all along, but somehow at the back of her mind she was starting to realize that she's been quite alone while she was going around the shops. She reminded herself that she'd found her child in the street, yet that explanation didn't quite sit right either, and after a few more seconds she felt a throbbing pain in the back of her head as she realized that she wasn't quite sure what had happened at all.

"You child-thieving wretch!" Mavis shouted, before stepping closer and spitting in her face.

"Stop it!" Katrina gasped, stepping back and wiping the blob of saliva from her cheek. "Please, I meant no harm. I think I just became confused for a moment, that's all."

"If you get confused again," Mavis hissed, "I'll be going to the police!"

With that, she turned and stormed away back up the beach, carrying her child as the others began to follow.

"I meant no harm!" Katrina sobbed again, even as she saw that several members of the little crowd were glancing back at her with puzzled – or in some cases hate-filled – expressions. "Please, just give me a chance to explain! I thought it was my own child, I thought that somehow he'd come back to me! I thought that someone or something had finally listened to my prayers!"

She waited, but now nobody was looking back at her and one-by-one the various locals began to disappear from view.

Dropping to her knees, Katrina put her hands over her face as she began to weep. For a few precious moments she'd managed to delude herself into believing that her child had been returned, but now she was under no illusion as to what had really happened; in a moment of madness she had simply snatched a child from the street, and soon the entire town would be talking about her. The worst part was that she couldn't even blame them: she knew that most of her remaining customers would soon desert her and that from now on she would barely be able to get by on the money she earned from the pub.

"I'm not a bad person," she whimpered as she watched waves crashing against the shore, before slowly getting to her feet. "I swear I'm not. I've always tried to do the right thing, it's just that lately my mind feels as if it's not quite my own. But I'd never do anything wicked, not intentionally. I just..."

In that moment, still watching the sea, she suddenly realized that she could feel another child in her arms. At first she was too scared to look down, but finally she forced herself to see: she was holding a bundle of cloths and blankets, and something inside that bundle was starting to wriggle. With a growing sense of hope in her heart, she began to pull one of the blankets aside – only to find herself staring down at a rancid mass of wriggling maggots.

"No!" she sobbed, throwing the bundle aside and turning to run, quickly falling and landing against the hard pebbles. "Please, don't make me see him like that!"

She couldn't help looking over her shoulder, however, but she immediately saw that the horrific sight was gone. Still out of breath and filled with panic, she looked around and saw that there was no-one else on the beach at all.

"I'm going to find you," she said under her breath, barely able to get any words out at all. "I don't know how, but I won't ever give up. And eventually, my darling boy, I'm going to get you back!"

CHAPTER EIGHTEEN

ONE MORE YEAR LATER, as the clock on the wall continued to tick, Katrina Mulligan stood behind the bar and stared at the window. She saw a few people wandering past the pub, but the days when regular visitors bothered to push open the front door were long gone. Now The Saracen's Head was lucky to receive more than a dozen customers each week, beyond the few locals who persisted.

"Another fine day out there," Ernest Townsend said, still sitting in the seat where – each and every day – he liked to peruse the newspaper while enjoying a pint of bitter. "I daresay there'll be mackerel for sale later. You can tell by the way the wind's blowing. Like myself a nice bit of mackerel, I do. Say, Katty, have you ever had mackerel with tomato?"

He let out a long, hungry sigh.

"That'll be my supper tonight, for sure," he added, looking out the window again. "I shall be glad to have a change from corned beef, that's for sure. I've been on the corned beef all week and there's nowt wrong with it, except a man likes a change now and again. You know where I'm coming from, Katty, don't you?"

"I should have found out its name," she whispered, having not even noticed that he was talking. "Then I could have called it back. Why didn't I find out the demon's name?"

"What's that?" Ernest asked. "I didn't quite catch what you were saying."

"But it's not too late," she added as tears glistened in her eyes. "It's *never* too late. I managed to make contact with something once, and I can do it again. I just have to make sure that it's the same demon and then I shall offer it whatever it wants. Any kind of -"

"Katty?"

Startled, she found that Ernest had made his way over and had set his empty glass on the bar.

"Sorry to disturb you, old girl," he continued with a faint smile, "but -"

"Get out," she stammered, suddenly filled with the need to go back to the cellar and try once more to reach out and contact whatever demon had stolen her child's corpse. "I'm closing early. Get out!"

"What do you mean?"

"Get out of the pub!" she snapped, hurrying out from behind the bar and pulling the door open. "You understand English, don't you? Get out and... and stay out! I've got too much to do, I can't be dealing with the likes of you, Ernest Townsend."

"Now listen here," he replied, stepping toward the door. "You don't have many regulars left here, Katty. You've driven most of 'em away and -"

"Out!" she yelled, pushing him through the open doorway with such force that he tripped and fell, landing with a thud on the pavement. "What's wrong with people? Why don't they ever listen?"

Without even stopping to check whether he was alright, she slammed the door shut and forced the bolt across. She didn't know it, but as she hurried away and rushed toward the steps leading down into the cellar, she had finally expelled her final customer from The Saracen's Head.

***

"Who are you?" she asked as she stood in the cellar, still a little breathless from the run down the stairs. "What do you want? I'll give you anything, you just... you just have to tell me."

Ahead, the cellar's floor was now a mess of

broken concrete, with thick cracks running in every direction. A stench of cold damp hung in the air as candles burned on a shelf, and Katrina could only stand in silence as she listened for any slight hint that she wasn't alone.

"Anything at all," she added, holding her hands up and admiring the many cuts and scars on her flesh. "I've given you blood. So much blood over the years. I don't know what else I have to offer, I have nothing as precious as my blood yet I would give my life if necessary. All that matters is that my child must find a way to live at least for a moment. I would give every remaining beat of my heart, just for his heart to beat once."

Again she waited for a response, but something about the cold cellar was almost screaming its emptiness back at her. How many hours had she spent on her hands and knees, desperately reaching down into the filthy mud beneath the concrete and searching for even a single bone from her child's fragile little body? Somehow the ground had swallowed him up entirely and she felt almost as if the dirt was mocking her, yet she'd never quite been able to abandon her mission. She knew she would never be able to rest while those bones were down there in the depths of the dark, godless soil beneath the building.

"I shall find another way," she murmured, turning to head back up the stairs. "If I have to find a shovel and dig until I lose all my strength then -"

In that moment, hearing another cracking sound, she turned to look back across the cellar. Sure enough, she saw that another crack was spreading across the floor; this was the first substantial new crack that had occurred in the five years since the initial damage had been caused.

"Are you here?" she called out, feeling a rush of hope in her heart. "Please, if you're here, say something!"

She waited, but already a sense of desperation was threatening to burst from her chest.

"Why won't you tell me what you want me to do?" she screamed. "Why won't someone just tell me how to get my son back?"

Again she waited, but this time the silence felt different; this time the silence felt intentional, almost defiant, as if the entire cellar had begun to hold its breath. For some time now, Katrina had felt sure that some other presence was lurking in the cramped space, but so far she'd always told herself to stop imagining such things. This time was different. This time she finally allowed her deepest and most paranoid fears to spill forth, until she found herself looking around the cellar and watching to see when the shadows might start to make their move.

"There's no point hiding," she purred. "Do you think that can possibly work?"

Determined to seem brave now, she took a step forward.

"Do you know where my parents came from?" she asked. "They came from the east, they were driven out of home after home. Eventually they reached Ireland, but even there they weren't safe. They were musicians, and finally they took the ferry over to Liverpool. They were hounded and hounded along every road, people spat on them because of who they were and what they looked like. They're long dead now, and fortunately I never experienced the treatment they were subjected to, but some of their resilience was passed down to me. I learned how to be strong, so you need to realize something... you will *never* break me. I will always -"

Before she could finish, she heard a faint squelching sound. She looked around, and soon she realized that the sound was coming from the deepest of the cracks on the floor.

Holding her breath, she told herself that there was no reason to be concerned. After a few more seconds, however, she realized that something was stirring in the depths, and she watched with a mounting sense of horror as a shape began to rise up slowly from the mud.

"Is it you?" she gasped, stepping forward in the hope that her child had finally returned. "Are -"

In that instant she saw that this was

something else entirely. A shape was indeed emerging from the bog of dirt and mud beneath the pub, but this shape was large enough to be that of a fully-grown man. With more and more mud dribbling down from all its sides, the figure began to rise up from the crack, seemingly able to hang in the air as it rose higher and higher. Eventually its head threatened to bump against the cellar's lower ceiling, and there the figure stopped as if it had finally reached its apogee.

Taking a few more faltering steps forward, Katrina suddenly felt all her bravery draining away. Although the creature before her was covered in all the filth and dirt and grime from beneath the building, as she stared up at its shape she felt as if she had come face to face with something ancient and powerful, with something that was stopping down for one moment and deigning to interfere in the realm of mortal men. And while she opened her mouth to once again ask this entity what it wanted and why it had taken her son, she was unsure that she even dared to speak to something so powerful.

"My... my child," she stammered. "I only... it's my child, that's all. I want my child back."

Tears were streaming down her face now and she felt she was closer than ever to her chance. Reaching out, she forced herself to touch the dripping figure.

"Please," she sobbed. "My child. I'll do

anything, just..."

As those words left her lips, she saw that the figure was slowly opening its mouth. As more and more mud dribbled away, she began to see the form beneath – and she felt her heart thudding to a violent halt as she found herself staring into the mouth of what she felt must surely be death itself.

CHAPTER NINETEEN

STUMBLING OUT OF THE pub, clutching her chest, Katrina looked around for help. The street was deserted in the late afternoon, and she could only take a couple more steps forward before dropping to her knees.

"Help me," she gasped, clawing at her chest now, threatening to rip the fabric away from her dress. "My heart, it stopped and..."

For a moment, blinking in the afternoon light, she thought back to the final seconds in the cellar. The mud-covered figure – a god, perhaps – had opened its mouth wider and wider, and finally Katrina had seen that it was holding something in its jaw, clenching a bundled shape between its ragged teeth. As a foul stench had emerged from the back of the figure's throat, Katrina had tilted her head slightly and had begun to understand what she was seeing in the creature's mouth.

And then she'd screamed.

"No!" she'd cried out, filled with a sense of panic. "My son! Don't -"

In that instant the figure had bitten down, crunching its teeth into the bundle. Hearing the sound of splitting bones, Katrina had screamed again, watching as blood had begun to dribble from the creature's mouth. She'd reached up and tried to tear her child from its mouth, but the creature had simply chewed for a few more seconds before reaching out with a clawed hand of its own and grabbing her left breast, squeezing tight and sending a shock-wave through her chest. And in that moment, still horrified by all the blood bubbling from the creature's mouth, Katrina Mulligan had felt her heart beat for the final time.

Somehow she'd made it back upstairs, forced onward by scraps of the bravery she'd claimed earlier. With the world spinning all around her, she'd somehow made it to the front door, which she'd ripped open in the vain hope that escaping from the pub might allow her to regain the use of her heart. Telling herself that she could recover and then return to find her son, she was on her knees now in the street and she began to frantically punch her own chest in a desperate attempt to force her heart to beat again.

"Help me," she groaned. "Somebody..."

Hearing footsteps, she turned and saw that two women had rounded the corner. Barely able to see properly, she reached out toward them. She saw the horrified expressions on their faces, but after a few seconds she was no longer able to hold herself up. Slumping down onto her side, she managed to force herself to roll over onto her back. Staring up at the pale sky, she opened her mouth in an attempt to call out to anyone nearby and warn them, but already her vision was fading and she could feel tears threatening to burst her eyeballs.

"Save him!" she tried to cry out. "Save... please... my son..."

All that emerged from her throat, however, was a series of guttural gasps, until finally she fell still. After a few more seconds one final clicking sound escaped from the back of her throat, but otherwise her body remained entirely motionless as deep inside her organs began to follow her heart into death. A few more people had gathered in the street now, but none of them dared to get too close to the death woman as the open door of The Saracen's Head swung gently in the wind and bumped against its frame.

***

2014...

"There was something down here," Rose whispered, staring at the cracks in the cellar floor as she felt Katrina Mulligan's echoing pain starting to fade. "It didn't like her very much. I think it was making fun of her."

"That was a very... gruesome story," Jonathan pointed out, watching her for a moment with a sense of concern before turning to his wife. "For an eleven-year-old."

"It certainly was," Rebecca said cautiously.

"Rose," Jonathan continued, "I hate to ask this but... Alicia hasn't been showing you any nasty films, has she? I know she tries to get into our stash of DVDs whenever we're out. Did Evelyn fall asleep again and let you girls into the cupboard?"

"How did you pick it all up?" Rebecca asked, placing a hand on Rose's shoulder. "It was very detailed."

"It's in the air," Rose explained, furrowing her brow a little. "I don't know how you *can't* pick it up. It happened here so... so it's still in the air. I don't know how else to say it."

"That's okay," Rebecca replied, turning to her husband again. "To me, it sounds like Katrina Mulligan was the victim of some kind of entity that was here in the cellar. Something seems to have been toying with her, perhaps even making her suffering worse on purpose. The poor woman must have been driven out of her mind by the end."

"Agreed," he said, nodding gently as he looked around the gloomy space. "At least we know now what happened to her child. It was sucked down beneath the building. That was already our assumption, but we can be sure of one thing. It's lost forever."

"Is it?"

He glanced at her again.

"A child's body would be light," she pointed out. "I don't see why it would necessarily end up being sucked deeper and deeper into the mud or -"

Stopping herself just in time, she looked down at Rose before getting to her feet. Leading Jonathan away slightly so that the girl wouldn't be able to hear, she also lowered her voice to a hush.

"We don't know that Rose was seeing exactly what happened," she whispered, "or whether she was witnessing everything through Katrina's perception."

"I'm not sure that I follow."

"If Katrina thought that she was seeing all manner of... strange creatures down here, then Rose might have been channeling all of that and seeing the madness herself. Doesn't that seem slightly more likely than the idea that some kind of... weird old god was summoned to the cellar of a pub?"

"Your guess is as good as mine right now," he admitted. "I'm starting to worry that we might be out of our depth."

"We need to see if we can find that child."

"But -"

"And you've got longer arms."

"What does that have to do with -"

Catching himself just in time, he began to understand exactly what his wife meant. He glanced at the crack in the floor for a few seconds, and when he turned to Rebecca again he realized that she was being serious.

"No way," he said. "Rebecca, are you kidding? We have no idea what's down there!"

"It's just mud," she told him. "And... dirt and soil and whatever. Do you remember that time you had to unblock the toilet?"

"Yes, but -"

"This really isn't any worse than that," she went on. "You'll just be reaching around under the concrete, it won't even take very long."

"I'm sure Katrina tried that," he suggested. "If she didn't find the remains of her child, then what hope do we have?"

"She was out of her mind," Rebecca pointed out, "and it was well over half a century ago. Jonathan, I know it's unlikely to work, but we have to at least try. I'm certain that if we can find the child's remains, we can deal with Katrina's ghost forever. As for the stuff about the weird figure emerging from the mud, I'm sure that was just a figment of her imagination." She paused for a moment, watching his face carefully. "But if you're scared, then I suppose I -"

"Who said I'm scared?" he asked quickly, as if he was offended by that idea.

"I just -"

"I can reach into some mud," he continued, although now he seemed to be trying a little too hard to make himself seem fine with the situation. A moment later he took off his jacket before starting to roll up his sleeves. "I'm not scared of a little hard work."

"I never said that you were."

"You think I'm some... stuffy academic who'd rather be sitting behind a desk than getting his hands dirty," he went on. "Literally. Well, Rebecca Pearson, I'm going to show you."

"I'm sure you are," she said with a wry smile.

"I'm a man of action," he added, "and if anyone can find that child's body down there in the mud, then it's going to be me." With that, he turned and made his way back over to the crack, before quickly getting down onto his knees and adjusting his sleeve again. "This is going to be really gross," he muttered in a moment of apparent realization, "but... if this is what it takes, then this is what it takes."

With that, he took a few more seconds to get

himself ready and then he slowly reached down and began to slide his right arm down into the cold mud.

CHAPTER TWENTY

YET ANOTHER SQUELCHING SOUND rang out across the cold cellar, accompanied by Jonathan's continued muttered complaints as he strained to reach deeper into the crack.

"Anything?" Rebecca called out to him.

"Give me a few more minutes," he replied. "There's a lot of... detritus under here. Twigs, pebbles, rocks... that sort of thing. It's actually thicker and more compacted than I expected."

Smiling, she turned to look over at Rose. In that moment she couldn't help but worry that she'd exposed the girl to too much drama, that she'd been acting selfishly when she'd driven home and literally dragged her out of bed. Ordinarily she'd never have done anything like that, of course, but something about the case of Katrina Mulligan was hitting her in a particularly personal way.

"Are you okay?" she asked finally.

Rose turned to her.

"I know it's late," she continued, "and you must be exhausted. I'm so sorry I brought you out here, Rose."

"Didn't I help?"

"Yes, but... that still doesn't mean I made the right decision."

"I get it," Rose said cautiously. "It must be harder for you. This case, I mean."

Rebecca hesitated, wondering exactly what the girl was trying to say.

"Do you miss him?" Rose asked.

"Miss who?"

"The..."

Now it was Rose's turn to hesitate, but after a moment she looked at Rebecca's belly.

"Your baby," she continued. "The one before Alicia. The one who died."

"How..."

Feeling as if her heart was racing now, Rebecca told herself that she had to remain calm and that she really needed to make sure that she didn't seem in any way flustered.

"Who told you about that?" she asked finally. "Alicia doesn't know... does she?"

"I don't think so," Rose replied.

"Did Jonathan tell you?"

Rose immediately shook her head.

"Then how did you know, Rose?" Rebecca continued, feeling both curious and also a little nervous. "It's okay, I won't be cross. I'm just really confused."

"I didn't realize it was a secret," Rose said timidly. "I just knew it."

"For how long?"

"I don't know."

"It's okay," Rebecca replied, struggling to hold back tears. "When did you first find out?"

"When I first met you," Rose admitted finally. "Back at Marlstone Hall. I didn't know it was a secret, I promise. I don't know why you think it's weird that I knew. I could tell just from looking at you." She paused, before slowly turning and looking over at Jonathan. "And I could tell from looking at him, too. You're both really sad about it, but in different ways."

Following the girl's gaze, Rebecca saw that her husband was still shoulder deep in the crack as he tried valiantly to find the child's corpse hidden deep in the depths. Her first instinct was to tell Rose that on this particular point she was wrong, that in fact Jonathan had managed to get past Alexander's death much more easily, but at the last second she held back as she began to realize that perhaps the girl was right after all. Just because he tended to avoid talking about what had happened, she understood now that this didn't necessarily mean that Jonathan had handled it any better.

"I -"

"I've got something!" Jonathan called out suddenly, wincing slightly. "I'm not sure what it is, but it feels different."

"I'm sorry," Rose whispered, bowing her head. "I didn't mean to make you even sadder."

"It's okay," Rebecca replied, feeling somewhat flustered as she got to her feet and hurried over to the crack. "What have you found?"

Behind her, Rose hesitated before suddenly turning and looking through a nearby archway, as if her attention had been grabbed by something elsewhere in the cellar.

"It's stuck," Jonathan muttered, pulling on whatever he'd found but so far not managing to get it to budge. "It might be snagged on something, or it might even be pressure. Whatever it is, though, it feels like something hard wrapped in some kind of fabric. Doesn't that sound like the body Katrina Mulligan lost?"

He pulled again and again, before letting out a frustrated sigh.

"I can't seem to get it to budge," he added. "I don't want to let go of it, either, in case I never find it again. Do you think you can find something we might be able to tie around it?"

"I'll try," Rebecca said, heading over to the

far side of the cellar. "I'm really not sure what we can use, but there might be something."

As she continued to search, Rose sat patiently in the corner near the steps. After just a few more seconds, however, she turned to look through the archway as she again heard something in some other part of the basement area. She hesitated, and then – after checking and seeing that both Rebecca and Jonathan were busy – she slowly got to her feet and stepped over to the archway so that she could listen a little better.

Once she managed to ignore Rebecca and Jonathan's conversation, she realized that she could hear a recurring clicking sound coming from somewhere nearby. As much as she wanted to tell herself that the sound was just some random noise burped up by an old building, deep down she already knew that it was being caused by something specific... or, rather, by *someone*. She hesitated, and then she glanced over her shoulder and saw that the others were busy, and then – telling herself that there was no harm in taking a look – she stepped through the archway.

***

"This isn't going to be easy," Jonathan said, taking the end of the rope his wife had found and starting to push it down into the mud, "but if I can wrap it around somehow, we might have a chance."

"Be careful," Rebecca cautioned him. "You don't want to break it."

"I know that," he murmured, clearly struggling to get both his hands deep enough into the space beneath the concrete floor. "I can't even be certain that it *is* the baby's body. It feels different to the other sticks I found, though. It's definitely something out of the ordinary."

Glancing over her shoulder, Rebecca saw that Rose was no longer by the bottom of the steps.

"Rose?" she called out. "Where are you?"

She waited, but she heard no reply.

"Jonathan, I think I should go and check on -"

"I've got it!" he gasped.

"Are you sure?"

"I've got the end of the rope around whatever it is," he muttered. "Just give me a moment. Can you pull a little harder on the rope? I'm worried that the whole thing might be too fragile and that we might not be able to pull it out without the whole bundle breaking. If it's been down in the mud for all these years, there's a chance it'll more or less just disintegrate as soon as we get it up."

Although she wanted to go and check on Rose, Rebecca told herself that the girl would be fine. Instead she focused on keeping her end of the rope tight, and she waited with baited breath as Jonathan continued to try to wrap it around whatever he'd found in the mud.

"Nearly there," he said under his breath, before finally pulling back slightly. "Okay, if you pull now, I'll try to keep it steady."

Rebecca immediately began to pull on the rope, although at first she felt as if she wasn't making any progress at all. Once Jonathan used his free hand to lift the rope slightly away from the edge of the crack, however, something deep in the mud began to shift and slowly but surely she was able to pull back. A couple of thick bubbles emerged from the depths and finally a small bulge began to break the surface of the mud.

"What is it?" Jonathan gasped. "Is it the baby?"

"I don't know," Rebecca replied. "It's too soon to tell. It's clearly quite substantial, though. Whatever it is, it must have been put down there by a person, and it's way too light to be a rock."

"We need to be careful," he continued. "The rope's already fraying on the concrete. It could break if we move too fast."

For the next couple of minutes, they worked slowly and methodically to extract the small bundle from the mud. Finally Jonathan was able to reach beneath it and pull it out properly, before setting it down onto the floor and starting to wipe away as much mud as possible.

"I still can't tell," he stammered.

"Where did Rose go?" Rebecca asked, setting the rope down before turning and looking back across the cellar. "Rose? Can you come back through? Rose, where are you?"

CHAPTER TWENTY-ONE

"ROSE? CAN YOU COME back through?" Rebecca's voice called out, echoing through the basement. "Rose, where are you?"

Having left the cellar area, Rose had now made her way through to another part of the basement entirely. Noticing a chill wind, she looked up and saw a hatch in the ceiling, and when she stopped beneath the hatch she was able to see the stars high above. The hatch itself led onto a long ramp made of bricks, and over at the far end of the ramp several large barrels had been left propped against the wall.

A moment later, just as she told herself that she should go back to Rebecca and Jonathan, the sound returned.

Standing completely still, Rose listened as a

baby's cry echoes in the air all around her, seemingly coming from every direction at once. She felt a shiver run through her bones, but after a few seconds the sound abruptly ended and was replaced by a series of occasional bumps and clicks.

"Is someone there?" Rose asked cautiously, not daring to raise her voice too high. "Is..."

As her voice trailed off, she realized that something felt very wrong. She was used to the sensation of noticing ghosts nearby, but this was different in a way that she wasn't quite able to understand. There was certainly a presence, of that she was absolutely certain, yet as she began to walk slowly toward another archway she felt as if this presence was in some way darker and more pressing than any she'd encountered before.

And more real.

Perhaps 'real' wasn't quite the right word, but as she stepped through another archway and entered a darker part of the basement, Rose couldn't work out exactly how to describe her senses.

"Rose?" she heard Rebecca shouting somewhere far away. "Can you come back please?"

She was aware of a dripping sound now, and as she ducked under a particularly low pipe she realized that she could no longer see where she was going. There was only darkness ahead, yet somehow Rose already knew that this part of the basement – the farthest part from the cellar area –

was clearly the focal point. Something was in this darkness, something that wanted to stay hidden, something that was staring back at her. Aware that she was probably silhouetted against the wall behind her, she was suddenly very much worried that she was out in the open. As much as she wanted to keep going, and to explore, she finally decided that she might need to employ some caution.

Slowly, she turned to go back the way she'd just walked. In that moment, however, an icy hand reached out from behind and clamped itself tight over her mouth.

***

"Sticks and rocks," Jonathan muttered as he continued to sort through the small bundle that he'd hauled up from beneath the concrete floor. "It looks like they've been tied together. You can't blame me for thinking that it was something else."

"I bet this belonged to Katrina Mulligan," Rebecca replied. "We know she tried all sorts of spells and incantations in an attempt to curry favor with spirits. I wouldn't be surprised if she spent lots of time crafting any type of... doll or other object that she thought might help."

"It's kind of pathetic," Jonathan pointed out.

"She was desperate," she replied, before glancing at him. "We both know how it feels to lose a child."

"Anyway, looks like we're done here," he said quickly, clearly wanting to change the subject as he folded the muddy fabric back around the paltry objects he'd recovered. "What should we do with this junk? Toss it back down there?"

"No idea," she said, before turning and looking toward one of the nearby archways, "but right now I'm more concerned about Rose. I haven't seen her for a while."

Stepping away from her husband, she approached the archway and looked through, but she saw only another of the basement's empty rooms.

"Rose?" she called out. "I know it's fun to explore, but I really need you to come back now. It's late and I ought to be getting you home."

She waited, but she heard nothing at all.

"She's probably just being a kid," Jonathan suggested. "If you ask me, we should just tell her we're leaving and go upstairs. She'll soon come out of the woodwork if she thinks she might get left down here."

"Rose, where are you?" Rebecca asked, before stepping through the archway. "Rose, I don't like the idea of -"

Suddenly Rose stepped into view ahead, seemingly a little startled.

"There you are," Rebecca said with a sigh,

gesturing for her to follow as she turned to head back to her husband. "Listen, it's getting late and we really ought to be getting out of here. We need to rethink our approach and come up with some other way to tackle whatever's going on."

Reaching the foot of the stairs, she stopped and looked back, only to see to her bemusement that Rose hadn't moved so much as an inch.

"Rose? What's wrong?"

The girl stared back at her for a moment before slowly turning and looking over her shoulder, as if watching something in some other part of the basement.

"Rose?" Rebecca continued. "Are you okay there?"

After staring back into the darkness for a moment, Rose finally turned and made her way through.

"I'm fine," she said, although she could barely look Rebecca in the eye now as she slipped past. "Can we go now? I'm cold down here."

"Not so fast," Jonathan said firmly. "We've got a lot of equipment down here. You can save me a double trip by helping to carry some up."

"She's exhausted," Rebecca pointed out, before taking Rose by the hand and leading her up the stairs. "Come on, you can sit in the car and wait while we tidy up down here."

Looking over her shoulder once again, Rose

seemed distinctly bothered by something, but she allowed herself to bed taken up into the pub's bar area.

"Actually," Rebecca continued, "why don't you just sit down here? I left the car a couple of streets away, parking's a nightmare round here. There's no need for us both to get cold, so just wait on one of these stools while I bring it round."

Obediently taking a seat, Rose watched as Rebecca left the building. Once the door was shut, she sat in silence for a moment as she contemplated the things she'd seen in the basement, until finally Jonathan made his way up with a couple of heavy boxes in his arms.

"See?" he said, carrying the boxes to the bar and setting them down. "Sometimes I think I'm no better than a donkey. I'm always the one who has to lug everything around."

"I don't mind helping," Rose said eagerly, getting to her feet again.

"Did Rebecca go to find the car?"

She nodded.

"There's one more box down there," he explained. "It's not heavy. I'll pop to the little boys' room while you fetch it, if you don't mind." He began to make his way toward the bathroom door. "You know, Rose, I think we might make a good little worker of you yet. You've got enthusiasm and that's one of the most important things. It certainly can't be taught."

He was still talking to himself as he headed into the bathroom.

Once she was alone, Rose waited for a few seconds before hurrying to the doorway that led down to the cellar. She looked toward the bottom and listened for a moment, and sure enough she soon heard the faintest hint of a baby crying. She glanced around, just to make sure that both Rebecca and Jonathan were otherwise engaged, and then she began to make her way down.

By the time she reached the bottom, she was almost shivering in the cold night air. The sound of the baby was intermittent at best, regularly cutting off for a few seconds at a time but inevitably returning fairly swiftly. Rose was so nervous now that she was almost holding her breath, but she told herself that she had to uncover the truth. A few seconds later, however, she heard a brief bubbling sound and she looked over just in time to see that the largest crack in the floor appeared to have been disturbed, with dirt splattered around the edges.

With the crying sound having stopped, at least for now, she made her way over and looked down into the crack, which if anything seemed even larger than before. Sure enough, a moment later one of the concrete sections shifted slightly, allowing the crack to grow just a little more; at the same time, a solitary bubble rose up through the murky liquid and appeared on the surface, although it was just a little too thick to burst just yet.

"Hello?" Rose whispered, kneeling down so that she could see into the crack a little better. "Is there anyone down there?"

As much as she wanted to go back through and find out some more about the baby, she couldn't shake the feeling that something important was down in the mud. She'd seen Jonathan reaching beneath the surface and she knew he hadn't managed to find anything, yet she also felt sure that there was something down in the depths. She leaned closer to the edge of the crack, watching the mud and waiting for some hint of a clue.

Suddenly a rotten hand reached down from behind, grabbing the back of her neck and immediately squeezing tight.

CHAPTER TWENTY-TWO

"I DON'T KNOW HOW people get by round here," Rebecca said as she stepped back into the pub. "The parking's a nightmare, I had to -"

Stopping suddenly, she saw that there was no sign of Rose on any of the stools. She spotted various boxes on the bar, and a moment later she heard a toilet flushing. A few seconds after that, still tightening his belt, Jonathan wandered out from the bathroom.

"There you are," he said. "Did you manage to get the -"

"Where's Rose?"

"She offered to fetch something from the basement," he replied, clearly not at all worried. "Listen, what are we going to do about old Derek upstairs? Leave a note? I've got a feeling that right now he'll have passed out after all that -"

"Rose?" Rebecca called out, trying not to panic as she hurried through to the hallway. Looking down into the cellar, she realized that she couldn't hear any hint of the girl at all. "Rose, are you down there? Rose, talk to me!"

"She's fine," Jonathan said cautiously, although he too was starting to wonder now. "She just went down to fetch a box."

He paused.

"That *was* a few minutes ago. But it was just a box and she's a curious kid. I'm sure she's perfectly okay."

"How could you let her go down there alone?" Rebecca asked, hurrying down the stairs. "Don't you realize that she's more susceptible to these things than the rest of us?"

"What do you mean by that?" he replied. "Rebecca? She just went to grab a box? How could she possibly get into trouble when she's just grabbing a box?"

He waited for a reply, but already he could hear his wife called Rose's name in the cellar. Convinced that at any moment the girl would respond, he hesitated, but after a few more seconds he began to feel a niggling sense of dread at the back of his mind. As much as he'd told himself that there was no real reason to worry, he was starting to think that maybe – just maybe – he might have made a mistake after all.

"She's fine," he stammered, before rushing down to join his wife. "She's a smart girl. There's nothing bad that could have happened to her! We don't have to overreact every single time she goes out of sight!"

***

"Rose?"

Stepping into another archway, Rebecca hesitated for a few seconds and listened to the ominous silence.

"Rose, this is no time for games," she continued as her husband finally joined her. "Rose, I need you to come out here right now! Do you understand? We're not angry at you, but you need to come with us! Rose, where are you?"

"This is crazy," Jonathan muttered. "I didn't think she could get into trouble fetching a simple box. People come down to this cellar all the time!"

"Not people like Rose," she replied, turning to him. "Don't you get it? Her connection to these entities isn't something she can just switch on or off at will. It's constant and she had no control over it at all!"

"Rebecca -"

"I think it's empathy," she added. "I might be wrong, it's just a working hypothesis, but I think

Rose has the most extraordinary sense of empathy that I've ever experienced in my life. She can read people like they're open books, she certainly read both of us, and I'm convinced that it's an ability that extends to the dead as well. In their case, it's so strong that she can actively read their lives somehow, as if she knows everything about them. And I'm worried that some of them, in turn, might recognize this in her and try to use it against her."

"Okay, now you're starting to sound a little crazy," he countered. "She's just a kid. A bright kid, but that's all."

"What about the card test?" she asked. "You said it yourself, when she was angry with you, she intentionally got every single card wrong!"

"I've been thinking about that," he replied, "and there might actually be a perfectly rational explanation for -"

Suddenly hearing a gasping sound, they both turned and looked back across the cellar. For a moment neither of them could quite work out what was happening, until a moment later a muddied hand broke out from beneath the concrete and tried desperately to grab onto the side. Unable to get any kind of purchase, the hand quickly began to sink back down, leaving a dirty trail.

"Rose!" Rebecca screamed, racing forward a fraction of a second before Jonathan realized what was happening.

Dropping down onto her knees, she plunged both hands into the crack, reaching so deep into the mud that she almost toppled forward. As Jonathan ran over and grabbed her from behind, determined to hold onto her, Rebecca continued to search desperately through the mud in an attempt to find the girl.

"She can't be down there!" Jonathan stammered. "What the hell would she be doing in the mud?"

"Let go of me!" Rebecca yelled, trying to push him away. "I can't get to her!"

"I'm not going to let you go in after her!" he hissed.

"It's my fault she's here!" she shouted, shoving him away more firmly before reaching deeper and deeper into the crack. "I think -"

In that moment she fell silent, before immediately starting to pull as hard as she could manage.

"Help!" she screamed. "Jonathan, help me get her out!"

Still not quite sure what was happening, Jonathan figured that his best bet was simply to do as he was told. He pulled on his wife as hard as he could manage, and slowly he was able to drag her back. After a moment he realized that she was holding onto something, and finally he watched as she hauled a small mud-covered figured out of the crack.

"Get water!" she shouted. "She can't breathe!"

Racing over to the barrels, he searched for anything he could use before grabbing a hose and pulling it away from the wall. Beer immediately began to spray from the end, but he figured that the had no time to come up with another plan; instead he turned and blasted both Rebecca and the figure on the ground with the jet, blasting all the mud away until at least he was able to see Rose curled up in a ball on the rough concrete.

"Stop!" Rebecca yelled.

Unable to simply turn the hose off, Jonathan tucked it behind one of the pipes.

"Rose, can you hear me?" Rebecca asked, reaching down and wiping matted hair from across the girl's face. "Rose, if you can hear me, say something."

For a fraction of a second Rose offered no response, before suddenly starting to cough violently. Still in a ball on the floor, with her arms wrapped around her chest, she brought up several mouthfuls of mud before starting to sit up, at which point she let her arms move down and a bundle of rags spilled out onto the ground. As it landed, the bundle fell apart and a set of old, stained bones tumbled into view – including what was clearly a small skull.

"Is that..."

Stepping closer, Jonathan couldn't quite believe what he was seeing.

"Is that it?" he asked. "Is that Katrina Mulligan's baby?"

"What were you doing down there?" Rebecca asked, helping Rose to sit up a little more. "Rose, I'm so sorry, I should never have left you alone, not even for a minute! Did something drag you under?"

Although she tried to respond, Rose immediately broke into another coughing fit. Rebecca began to pat her back hard, as Jonathan crouched down and began to sort through the various bones.

"They're not in bad condition," he pointed out. "They're remarkably well-preserved, although I'd hazard a guess that the composition of the soil played a big role in that. It looks like all the flesh is gone, and the hair as well, but let's not forget that this child has been dead for the best part of three quarters of a century. All things considered, this isn't bad going."

He held up the skull.

"It's so small," he pointed out. "After all these years, the poor little thing has finally been hauled back up into the light. I can't believe no-one managed to find him before. I searched and searched but I didn't have any luck. Rose, exactly how deep were these bones?"

"We found him," Rebecca said, still patting Rose hard on the back as she began to look around the room, watching for any sign that the ghostly figure of Katrina Mulligan might return. "Do you think that's it? Is that enough? Will she stop haunting the pub now?"

CHAPTER TWENTY-THREE

"DON'T YOU THINK THIS is slight overkill?" Jonathan asked a few minutes later, following along the dark and deserted street as Rebecca and Rose hurried hand-in-hand toward the cemetery. "Like you said just now, it's probably all fine now."

"I'm sticky," Rose said, licking her lips again. "Really sticky. Is this beer?"

"Don't lick it," Rebecca replied firmly.

"But -"

"I'm telling you, Rose," she added, briefly glaring at her as they made their way through the gate at the front of the cemetery. "I'm already on the hook for some pretty major neglect tonight. Let's not have you getting drunk on top of it all."

"It doesn't even taste nice," Rose commented. "Why would anyone want to drink it?"

"Here's the grave," Jonathan said, stopping in front of the stone bearing the names of Katrina Mulligan and her husband Stephen. "I suppose they're both down there, resting in peace, but can we really just dig a hole and throw the baby in? That seems somewhat... basic."

"Do you have any better ideas?" Rebecca asked, carefully setting the bundle of bones on a nearby tomb before grabbing the shovel her husband had borrowed from the pub's garden. "I have no idea how hallowed ground even works, but it seems to be important to the dead. There'll be time to figure all of that out later, but right now we need to bury the child properly."

As Jonathan took the shovel, insisting that he should be the one to do the hard labor, Rose turned and looked toward the gate. She could see a row of shops opposite the cemetery, but all the lights were off. Stepping back over to the gate, she looked along the street and saw some kind of modern art gallery and – a little further away – a shuttered Thai restaurant. Something about the scene made her feel more than a little nervous, however, even as she watched the shadows and spotted no sign of anything untoward.

"How deep does it have to be?" Jonathan asked. "Don't you think this should be enough?"

"A fox would easily get it if it's not deeper," Rebecca told him.

"Then how deep are we going?" he continued, sounding increasingly exasperated. "We're not going to try for a full six feet, are we?"

Barely even noticing their voices, Rose stepped a little further away from the gate until she was standing on the edge of the pavement. She looked back the way they'd just run, and she thought of The Saracen's Head waiting out there in the darkness. A moment later, however, she spotted something moving in the distant shadows, and she immediately flinched as she realized that a female figure was slowly but surely making its way closer.

"Foxes won't bother digging up dried old bones," Jonathan was insisting now. "They want meat!"

"We can't be sure," Rebecca insisted. "If you don't want to keep digging, then give me the shovel and I'll get the hole done."

"I didn't say that," he said with a heavy sigh. "I'm just not quite sure that we need to be expending so much energy."

"Rebecca?" Rose said cautiously, as the shadowy figure briefly disappeared before emerging once more near the Thai restaurant. "Jonathan? I don't think we're alone."

"Won't the fabric help?" Jonathan asked wearily. "Hell, why don't I wrap the bones in my coat? That way there's no way a fox'll be able to smell what's down there."

"Their senses of smell are a little stronger than that, Rebecca countered.

"Then what do you suggest?" he continued.

"Jonathan?" Rose said, taking a step back as the shadowy figure began to cross the street, heading slowly toward the cemetery. "Rebecca, I think the ghost from the pub is coming after us."

"Hang on, Rose," Jonathan said. "We're talking. Just let -"

"What did you say?" Rebecca asked, hurrying over to the girl and looking out at the street.

"I -"

In that moment, Rose realized that the ghostly figure – which had certainly looked a lot like the woman from the pub's cellar – was now nowhere to be seen.

"It's alright," Rebecca said, putting a hand on her shoulder. "We won't let her get to you again. I know it must have been scary when she pushed you into the mud, but you won't ever go into that basement again."

"She didn't push me," Rose replied, looking up at her.

"What do you mean?" Rebecca asked. "Of course she pushed you. How else could you have ended up down there?"

"She didn't push me," Rose continued cautiously, as if she was scared to tell the truth. She looked over at Jonathan for a moment, then back at Rebecca. "I *wanted* to go in and find her baby for her."

***

Fifteen minutes earlier...

"Hello?" Rose whispered, kneeling down so that she could see into the crack a little better. "Is there anyone down there?"

As much as she wanted to go back through and find out some more about the baby, she couldn't shake the feeling that something important was down in the mud. She'd seen Jonathan reaching beneath the surface and she knew he hadn't managed to find anything, yet she also felt sure that there was something down in the depths. She leaned closer to the edge of the crack, watching the mud and waiting for some hint of a clue.

Suddenly a rotten hand reached down from behind, grabbing the back of her neck and immediately squeezing tight. Startled, Rose pulled away and spun around, tripping in the process and landing hard on the concrete floor.

Staring up into the darkness, she was horrified to see a pale, dead woman standing above her. Intermittently fading and then returning, the woman was sobbing as she reached out again with her withered hand. This time, feeling less scared, Rose watched the woman's face for a few seconds before looking once more into the crack.

"He's down there," she said softly. "Isn't he? You were right all along, but you couldn't get to him. Neither could Jonathan."

As she began to hear the sobbing now, which seemed to be breaking through from another world, she crawled to the edge of the crack and looked down. She thought for a moment, and finally she understood exactly what she had to do.

"I see him," she whispered. "No, I can't *see* him, but I know where he is. He's just out of reach, but not by much. I think..."

She paused, before sliding her legs around and dipping them into the cold mud. She winced as soon as she felt the icy liquid against her skin, but she knew that she had to help the ghostly woman. For a few seconds she was again able to hear the cries of a child echoing all around, until finally she began to lower herself into the crack.

"I'll find him," she continued, trying to ignore the immense sense of fear that even now was spreading through her chest. "I don't know how, but I know exactly where he is."

Keeping hold of the side of a concrete block in an attempt to steady herself, Rose lowered herself even further until finally she was submerged up to her neck. She knew she needed to go a little deeper in order to get hold of the bones, and she was starting to realize that this meant she was going to have to dip her face under the water. As much as she hated that idea, she could feel the ghostly woman's grief hanging in the air all around and she knew that she couldn't let such suffering continue.

"Okay, I'll be really quick," she stammered, delaying the moment for a little longer. "Be brave, Rose. Be really brave. Be braver than you've ever been in your life."

Finally she forced her head under while keeping one hand on the edge of the concrete. Once she'd disappeared from view, only her hand remained until this too slid beneath the surface. A couple of thick bubbles escaped to the top of the mud, but already there was no sign of Rose at all, even as footsteps hurried down the stairs from higher up in the pub.

"Rose, are you down here?" Rebecca called out, looking around the cellar but seeing no sign of the girl, and not noticing the ghostly woman who even now was still waiting at the edge of the crack.

"Rose?"

Stepping into another archway, Rebecca hesitated for a few seconds and listened to the ominous silence.

"Rose, this is no time for games," she continued as her husband finally joined her. "Rose, I need you to come out here right now! Do you understand? We're not angry at you, but you need to come with us! Rose, where are you?"

CHAPTER TWENTY-FOUR

Fifteen minutes later...

"YOU WENT DOWN THERE on purpose?" Rebecca stammered, barely able to believe the story she'd just heard. "But Rose, that's... I mean, are you crazy? You could have been killed!"

"I was trying to be brave," Rose replied with tears in her eyes. "I'm sorry, I didn't mean to be bad."

"You weren't bad," Rebecca told her, dropping to her knees and putting her hands on the girl's shoulders, "but you have to understand just how dangerous that was. What if you'd got lost in the mud?"

"How would I get lost in the mud?"

"You could have lost your bearings. You

might have become disorientated. Rose, a million things could have gone down there and you would have run out of air!"

Rose thought about that for a moment, before shaking her head.

"I knew where the bones were," she explained, "and I knew where the top was. I don't know how, but I just did. And it was cold and yucky, but the dead woman in the cellar was so upset and I knew I was probably the only one who could get her baby's bones back up. Should I have waited for you? I don't think you'd have been able to find them."

"You're not in trouble," Rebecca told her once more, "just... try to not dive into situations like that again, okay? You were extremely brave and you did a good thing, but you mustn't put yourself in danger in the process. And you mustn't keep things from us, either. Do you understand, Rose? If anything like that happens again, instead of taking matters into your own hands, you must tell either Jonathan or myself immediately."

"But then she'd still have been sad."

"I'm not sure she's in the greatest mood *now*," Jonathan said, grabbing Rebecca's arm. "She's here!"

Turning, Rebecca and Rose both saw what he meant: the ghostly figure of Katrina Mulligan had walked slowly past them and was approaching the bag of bones on a nearby tomb. Before anyone could say anything, Katrina reached down with a pale hand and began to move the edges of the fabric aside before very slowly holding up a collection of bones, including the skull.

"That's her," Rebecca said as she felt a tightening sense of fear in her chest. "That's Katrina!"

"I didn't think she'd be able to leave the pub," Jonathan replied.

"It's the bones she's haunting," Rebecca explained, "not the pub itself. I bet she doesn't give a damn about the pub, not any more. All she cares about is the bones of her long-dead son."

Rose pulled back slightly, almost hiding behind Rebecca but in the end forcing herself to watch as the ghostly figure tilted its head and examined the bones more closely.

"That's great," Jonathan said, "but what do -"

Suddenly the bones began to crumble away, turning to dust and then blowing into the night wind. A fraction of a second later, before anyone else had a chance to react, Katrina screamed and pulled away, and in that moment she too faded away into the darkness as the last of the dust fell down and settled on the cold grass.

***

"Was that a happy ending?" Rose asked as she sat on a nearby bench, shivering slightly as she watched Jonathan patting the freshly-laid soil on the grave. "It didn't seem very happy."

"I'm sure -"

Before she could get another word out, Rebecca realized that perhaps there was no point lying to Rose. She'd been able to tell her that the ghost of Katrina Mulligan could rest now, yet that final scream still seemed to linger somehow in the air. Deep down, Rebecca couldn't shake the feeling that the woman had suffered so much and for so long that there had been no possibility of an entirely happy conclusion to the sorry affair. Instead, at best, Katrina's long suffering was finally over and she could hopefully rest in peace.

Anything else was surely a little too far out of reach.

"She's moved on now," she said finally. "Before you ask, I don't know where she might have gone, but at least she's not here and... I hope she'd not hurting."

She looked down at Rose, and in that moment she realized that she'd made the right decision. The girl was clearly far too intelligent and perceptive to believe any fumbled attempts to sanitize the truth.

"We can't undo bad things that happened in

the past, Rose," she explained. "Not completely. We can only do our best."

"But was that really Katrina Mulligan?" Rose asked. "Did she think and feel? Or was it... I don't know, was it just part of her that got left behind?"

"That's a very good question," Rebecca admitted, "and unfortunately at the moment I'm afraid I can't answer it. That's one of the many things that Jonathan and I are trying to work out."

"I could only feel sadness in her," Rose replied. "She didn't even have any hope. She was just really sad and she could only think about the baby. Nothing else seemed important to her."

"That must be a horrible way to exist," Rebecca suggested, before tousling the hair on top of the girl's head. "Young lady, you're soaked and it's cold and we really need to get you home. This has definitely not been my finest moment since you came to live with us."

"It's okay," Rose said, "I understand. You were both probably thinking about..."

Again, her voice trailed off.

"Can I ask you a question?" she continued finally.

"Shoot," Rebecca replied, still impressed by the girl's emotional intelligence.

"Why doesn't Alicia know she had a brother?" Rose asked. "I mean... why doesn't she know that she *almost* had a brother? Is it because you're scared of upsetting her?"

"Something like that," Rebecca admitted.

"I think I'd want to know," Rose went on. "But you probably know better."

"I'm not so sure about that," Rebecca replied. "I'll give your question some real thought. Alicia's getting older now, so the time might have come for us to be a little more honest with her."

"Maybe," Rose said, before offering a shrug. "I don't know."

"So the grave's done," Jonathan said, trying to hide a slight sense of breathlessness as he made his way over, carrying the shovel in a somewhat triumphant manner. "I compromised and put what remained of the bones about three feet down. To be honest, I'm really not sure that it's going to make a huge difference. No foxes are going to be interested and, beside, it looks like Katrina Mulligan is finally out of the picture. I hope she is, anyway."

"Now we really *should* be getting back," Rebecca suggested, getting to her feet and gesturing for Rose to do the same. "We're all going to be really tired in the morning."

"Do you think everyone at The Saracen's Head will be okay?" Rose asked.

"I'll give Derek a call in the morning," Rebecca continued, "but I don't see why they shouldn't be. With Katrina's ghost hopefully gone, they might be able to start getting back to normal. I'll suggest that they need to fix that broken floor, though. Even with the child's bones gone, we don't want anyone to be tempting fate."

As they walked out through the gate, Rose remained locked in thought for a moment.

"I understand," she said cautiously, "but what about the other baby?"

"What other baby?" Rebecca asked absent-mindedly, barely even taking any notice.

"The other baby in the cellar."

Stopping, Rebecca and Jonathan both turned to her.

"What about the other baby?" Rose continued. "I know it doesn't cry all the time, but it still cries *sometimes*, and I'm worried that it's sad. Or... not sad, exactly, but scared. I don't think it quite understands what's happening."

"There's no other baby in the cellar," Jonathan told her. "There was only one, and we got rid of it."

"But what about the other one?" Rose asked.

"What other one?" Rebecca replied, crouching in front of her and looking deep into the girl's eyes. "Rose, I'm sorry but I really don't quite follow you. Katrina Mulligan only lost one baby."

"I know," Rose said matter-of-factly.

"And we buried that baby now," Rebecca continued. "What was left of it, at least."

"I know," Rose said again.

"So then... what baby are you talking about?"

Rose hesitated, looking first at Rebecca and then at Jonathan – and then back at Rebecca again.

"I mean the other baby in the cellar," she explained finally, as if that was the most obvious answer in all the world. "That one that's still alive. Haven't you noticed it?"

"Noticed what?" Rebecca asked.

"The other baby in the cellar," Rose said again, sounding a little more frustrated this time. "The one that's not dead. How can you not have noticed it? Jane, the landlord's daughter, has a new baby and she's been keeping it hidden in the cellar!"

CHAPTER TWENTY-FIVE

Earlier...

"ROSE?" SHE HEARD REBECCA shouting somewhere far away. "Can you come back please?"

She was aware of a dripping sound now, and as she ducked under a particularly low pipe she realized that she could no longer see where she was going. There was only darkness ahead, yet somehow Rose already knew that this part of the basement – the farthest part from the cellar area – was clearly the focal point. Something was in this darkness, something that wanted to stay hidden, something that was staring back at her. Aware that she was probably silhouetted against the wall behind her, she was suddenly very much worried that she was out in the open. As much as she wanted to keep going, and to explore, she finally decided that she might need to employ some caution.

Slowly, she turned to go back the way she'd just walked. In that moment, however, an icy hand reached out from behind and clamped itself tight over her mouth.

"What the hell are you doing down here?" a voice hissed.

Struggling to break free, Rose could already tell that she was being held far too firmly in an almost vice-like grip.

"I should have known there'd be trouble," Jane Handley continued. "I tried to play nice, I tried to help those idiots and make them move on, but they just had to keep poking around."

She paused for a moment.

"I'm gonna let go of your mouth, little girl," she added, "but if you scream or make any kind of noise to attract attention, I'll... I'll kill you. Got it?"

Rose nodded frantically.

After hesitating for just a couple more seconds, Jane let go and shoved Rose forward, sending the girl stumbling against the opposite wall. As soon as she turned, Rose saw genuine fear in the older girl's eyes, and a moment later – sensing just the faintest noise – she looked at the half-open door of a nearby cupboard.

"You can't say anything," Jane went on. "No-one knows, and it's gonna stay that way."

Although she opened her mouth to ask what Jane meant, after a fraction of a second Rose realized that she didn't really need to ask that question. Instead, hearing the sound of fabric shifting, she stepped toward the cupboard and gently pulled the door open, and then she let out a gasp as soon as she spotted a newborn baby in a set of blankets.

"She's three weeks old," Jane continued as tears began to fill her eyes. "It's not my fault, okay? It just... it happened. I went out one night to find Mum when she was on another of her benders, and there were some guys who were trying to help her. They were in a band that had been playing in the pub. One thing led to another, and nine months later..."

Her voice trailed off for a moment.

"The craziest part is that I don't even remember what the band was called," she added, sniffing back tears now. "I'm not sure I could track him down, even if I wanted to. It's so typical, isn't it? I was probably just some sad little groupie to him, just some easy girl in a boring town. I bet it happens to him all the time. But for me, it changed everything."

As soon as the baby began to gurgle, Jane rushed over and dropped down onto her knees.

"Don't make a sound," she said urgently. "Mummy's here."

"Is that really *your* baby?" Rose asked.

"Don't judge me," Jane said through gritted teeth. "Everything anyone could possibly call me, I've already thought of." She adjusted the blankets to keep the child a little warmer. "I managed to hide the pregnancy. I didn't show much, and Mum and Dad aren't exactly the most observant parents in the world. And I was lucky, I went into labor while they were both out and there were no complications. Since then I've been keeping her hidden down here while I try to work out what to do next. I hate the idea of giving her away, but I know that might be best for her. She can't stay down here like this and Mum and Dad'll flip when they find out what I've done."

The baby gurgled again.

"I hate it when she cries and I have to put my hand over her mouth," Jane sobbed. "I hate it! I hate it! I hate it! But I don't know what else to do. I keep telling myself that I'm not going to get too attached to her, that I won't even name her." She paused again. "But her name's Lucy. I don't know why, it just is. And I'm the worst mother anyone could ever have in the whole world."

Although she wanted to say something, Rose instinctively understood that she was way out of her depth and that she couldn't possibly think of any words that would make the situation better. She still didn't quite understand how someone like Jane could have had a baby of her own, and the idea scared her a lot, but a few seconds later she heard Rebecca calling out for her again and she realized that she needed to get back to the cellar.

"Don't tell anyone!" Jane hissed, turning to her again. "I mean it! I'll sort this out, I swear. I won't keep hiding her for much longer. I might leave her on a step at the hospital or something like that, I just... I can't do it quite yet." She looked back down at the baby and gently ran a finger against the side of her face. "Not yet," she whimpered as fresh tears ran from her own eyes. "Just promise me you won't tell anyone. I need time, that's all. I need time to figure out what the hell I'm supposed to do next."

***

Later...

"I can't believe a girl like Jane could hide a baby in

a pub," Rebecca said breathlessly as she hurried across the dark street, heading back toward The Saracen's Head. "How oblivious can her parents be?"

"They're a pair of drunks," Jonathan pointed out as he and Rose followed. "Let's call a spade a spade here. There's no way people like the Handleys should be running a pub."

Reaching the front door, Rebecca grabbed the handle to push it open, only to find instead that it was somehow now locked. She tried a couple more times before taking the key from her pocket, but even this failed to work and she quickly realized that someone had slid the bolt across on the inside.

"We're locked out!" she snapped, unable to hide a sense of frustration. "Why would Derek do that?"

"I doubt he did," Jonathan said, looking up at the pub's higher windows. "I'm pretty sure he's passed out in front of the telly after drinking himself stupid. I doubt he'd got any clue about anything that's been going on here tonight... or any other night, for that matter."

"Then we need to wake him up," Rebecca said firmly.

"Why don't you use the trap door?" Rose asked.

They both turned to her.

"It's right around the corner," the girl continued, pointing past them both. "I don't think it's locked from the inside. I noticed earlier."

"You've very observant," Rebecca pointed out.

"I just notice things," Rose said, as if that was the most natural thing in the whole world. "Don't *you*?"

Hurrying around the corner, Rebecca quickly found the hatch in the pavement. Crouching down, she found that – sure enough, just as Rose had predicated – it opened easily, allowing her to look down into the darkness of the pub's cellar.

"I can hear something," she said after a moment. "Someone's talking, but I can't quite make out what they're saying."

"They're not talking," Rose whispered. "It's different. It's like..."

She thought for a moment, trying to think of the right word.

"Chanting," she added finally.

"I'm going down," Rebecca said, swinging her legs over the side. "Stay up here with Rose."

"Actually," Jonathan replied, "I think it might be better if I'm the one who -"

Before he could get another word out,

Rebecca began to scramble down into the darkness, struggling to navigate the deep incline that led into the area beneath the pub. She was quickly out of view, however, leaving Jonathan and Rose standing on the pavement and listening to the sound of her efforts.

"Shouldn't we go down and help her?" Rose asked after a moment.

"I can't exactly leave you up here all alone in the middle of the night," he pointed out. "I'm sure nothing's wrong, though. The ghost of Katrina Mulligan should be long gone now. It's just a matter of making sure that Jane and her baby get the help they need."

CHAPTER TWENTY-SIX

AS SOON AS SHE dropped down into the dark basement and switched her flashlight on, Rebecca realized that Rose had been absolutely correct.

Someone nearby was chanting.

For a moment, not daring to move, she simply remained in position near the bottom of the slope and listened as the voice continued. Quickly realizing that she couldn't quite make out any of the words, however, she began to inch forward through the cramped space while taking care to angle the flashlight's beam down in an attempt to avoid being spotted too easily. By the time she reached the next archway, however, she was just about able to hear some of the words that were being called out somewhere nearby.

"I'm offering you what you've always

wanted," the young female voice was saying. "I know it's how *she* contacted you all those years ago. And if she could do it, then... then so can I. Especially when I've got something more important than she could ever give you."

A moment later, as if on cue, a baby began to gurgle slightly.

"This baby's alive," the voice continued. "Not like that stupid bitch all those years ago offering up a corpse. How did she ever think that a dead baby would achieve anything? She was pathetic. But me..."

Again the voice hesitated for a few seconds.

"I'm offering you this living baby," the girl added finally. "You can do what you want with it. I really don't care. All I ask in return is that you give me everything I've ever wanted. I've sensed your power. Even after all these years, some part of you is still down here in this stinking place, isn't it? You came here for that dead bitch all those years ago but I know you can still hear me. And I know we can strike a deal."

Confused, Rebecca ducked under the archway and made her way forward. Spotting flickering candlelight ahead, casting ever-changing shadows against the wall, she figured that she needed to be a little more circumspect. She switched her flashlight off before edging closer, although after a moment her left foot bumped against something hard on the floor. Looking down, she was shocked to see a human figure slumped on the concrete.

"I don't know exactly *how* you want it," the voice went on, as Rebecca slowly crouched down. "I thought you'd be okay to just take it like this, but maybe not. That's okay, though. I've... I've got what I need right here to get the job done properly."

As she tried to make sense of those words, Rebecca slowly began to roll the collapsed figure over. To her surprise, she found herself looking down at Jane Handley, and a bloodied cut on the girl's forehead suggested that she'd been knocked out by a hefty blow.

"Jane," Rebecca whispered, nudging her shoulder gently in an attempt to rouse her. "Can you hear me? Jane, are you okay?"

She waited, but the girl showed no sign that she was about to stir from her state of unconsciousness. Checking the side of her neck, Rebecca quickly determined that the girl was at least still alive, although the blow to her head had clearly been enough to knock her out cold for quite a while.

"Jane," she said again, before realizing that she probably wasn't going to have much luck. "Wait here," she added, slowly getting to her feet as she turned and looked toward the main part of the cellar, where the candles continued to flicker. "I think -"

Before she could finish, someone grabbed her from behind and spun her around, quickly slamming her hard against the cellar's brick wall.

***

"I'm cold," Jonathan muttered, and sure enough he was shivering slightly as he stood on the street round the side of The Saracen's Head. "Are you okay in Rebecca's coat?"

Staring into the darkness beyond the cellar door, Rose took a few seconds to even notice that he'd said anything. When she looked up at him she still struggled to make sense of the words she'd heard, since she felt as if something else – something far more important – was reaching out and very gently tugging at the edge of her mind. The strangest part of the whole sensation, however, was that this 'something else' didn't seem to be coming from the pub at all, and instead was emanating from somewhere further back along the street.

"Rose?" Jonathan said cautiously. "Are you okay?"

"I don't think we should be here," she replied.

"I can certainly agree with you on that," he said with a faint smile as he checked his watch.

"This was supposed to be a quick one day job and instead -"

"No," she said, cutting him off, "I mean I don't think we should be *here*. Where we're standing."

Puzzled, he looked down at his feet, then at her feet, and then he met her gaze again.

"Okay," he continued, "even by your standards, that's a slightly odd thing to say. Would you mind elaborating a little?"

He waited, but now Rose was peering past him and seemed more focused on the road leading toward the cemetery. Following her gaze, Jonathan felt a shiver run through his bones as a chill wind blew against him, but otherwise there was nothing obviously amiss and he quickly told himself that the girl was probably just allowing her imagination to run rampant. After all, she'd been through a great deal.

"I wouldn't worry too much," he told her. "Let's just -"

"She's coming back!" she gasped.

"Who is?" he asked, looking down into the cellar. "Do you mean -"

"I thought she was going to stay in the graveyard!" Rose stammered, stepping back until she bumped against the wall. "Why is she coming back *here*?"

"Do you mean the ghost of Katrina

Mulligan?" he replied. "Rose, I don't see anyone. I think you might be imagining things."

"She's coming this way!"

Again he looked along the street, and again he saw absolutely no sign that anyone – alive or dead – might be on their way. He opened his mouth to tell Rose that she could relax, but when he glanced down at the girl again he saw that she was absolutely terrified. Sure enough, just a moment later she stepped behind him and gripped his hand as if she was trying to hide.

"Rose, this is getting a little silly," he continued. "Why would Katrina Mulligan's ghost ever want to come back to the pub now? She has her baby, we reunited them. If you just think about it logically, there's no reason why she should ever come here again. I'm sure she's moved on to... I don't know, to wherever ghosts go once they retire from the haunting game."

"She's crossing the road," Rose said, and now her voice was trembling with fear.

"I don't see anyone," he replied with a hint of desperation in his voice. "Rose -"

"I don't want to see her again," Rose continued, pulling on his hand as if she was desperately trying to get him away from the hatch. "She's going to go back down there. Please, we can't be standing here when she reaches us. We have to move!"

"Rose, I appreciate that you have a certain degree of sensitivity when it comes to these things," he said, "but I don't think it'd be wise of me to indulge you right now. You need to recognize that sometimes it's quite possible to have your imagination run riot, and you need to learn when to keep hold of things a little more. Do you understand where I'm coming from?"

"Please, you have to move," she whimpered, pulling hard and harder on his hand. "Jonathan, she's nearly here! She looks so scary!"

Again he looked around, and again he saw no sign whatsoever of the ghostly figure. As much as he tried to remind himself that there might still be a danger, when he looked down at Rose again he felt sure that she was simply letting her childish imagination off the leash, and that this was an important chance to teach her the value of self control. All he had to do, he figured, was try to instill in the girl some sense of awareness so that she -

Suddenly he let out a gasp as he felt an icy chill pass straight through his body from the back to the front. Stumbling to one side, he let go of Rose's hand and tried to speak, but at the last second he spotted a dark shape stepping away and starting to move slowly down into the cellar. And then, before he had a chance to say another word or to warn Rose, he felt his legs give way and he passed out, slamming down hard against the cold pavement.

CHAPTER TWENTY-SEVEN

"I WAS HOPING IT wouldn't come to this," the girl's voice said nervously, still echoing through the cellar, "but... I get it. You want some kind of sign that I'm willing to do absolutely anything for you. I guess this is the only sign that'll really be big enough."

Struggling to get free, Rebecca felt heavy arms still wrapped tight around her, keeping her from fully turning around. After a moment she felt hot breath against the side of her neck, and she half-turned as she realized that she could hear someone grunting nearby.

"What are you doing down here?" a male voice snarled. "Are you trying to stop us?"

"Who are you?" Rebecca stammered.

"Does that even matter?" he replied as the

girl continued to chant in the next part of the cellar. "What we're doing here tonight is bigger and more important than anyone else could ever realize. Jessie made contact with something down here and now she's going to find it again, and this time she's going to make sure that it sees her true potential."

"Jessie?" Rebecca replied, trying to remember where she'd heard that name before. "Wait, do you mean the girl who broke into the cellar a few months ago and -"

"There's something in this cellar," he snarled. "Something far bigger than any of us. And Jessie made me see that we need to be the first to make proper contact, because then we can show that we'll help. That way, when this thing comes through properly to claim the world, we'll be in the small group of people who get saved. We even know this entity's name now. Jessie did loads of research and she narrowed it down, she's certain that it's Vecsael."

"What are you talking about?" Rebecca asked, trying to play for time as she worked on a plan to get away from the guy's clutches. "What's Vecsael?"

"She's some kind of ancient priestess," he explained. "All those years ago, when Katrina whatshername begged for help in this cellar, the spirit of Vecsael was accidentally summoned. But when you do something like that, when you open a door that's so important, you can't expect it to just shut again. Those doors stay open, and that's why even after so many years Jessie's going to find a way to make contact again. Even if it's been decades in our world, for the entities on the other side of that door, it's only been like the blink of an eye."

"Is that right?"

"That's right," he said confidently. "You can't mess around with things like this. You have to really know what you're doing and -"

"Taylor?" the girl's voice called out suddenly. "Hey, are you coming? I need your help, I don't think I can do this part alone. It's kinda turning out to be much harder than I expected."

"I've got to go to her now," he muttered. "Listen, if -"

Suddenly Rebecca threw all her weight against him, shoving him hard against the other wall. Feeling his grip loosening, she reached out and grabbed the old shovel she'd spotted propped against the wall and she swung the handle, smashing it against the side of Taylor's head and knocking him out. Breathless now as she took a step back, she watched as he slumped down against the concrete floor.

"Taylor?" Jessie shouted from the basement. "Taylor, seriously, we need to get on with this. I think something's close, but we have to show it that we mean business. We need to make a sacrifice! We need to prove that we're worthy!"

***

"Jonathan, are you okay?" Rose asked, dropping onto her knees as she nudged him. "Jonathan, can you say something? Please? I told you not to stand there, I told you she was coming back. Why wouldn't you listen to me?"

She waited, but she could already tell that he was out cold.

Swallowing hard, she looked down into the cellar again. She'd heard voices just a moment earlier and on some deep level she could already sense that Rebecca was in trouble, but for a few seconds she wasn't quite sure how to respond. The ghostly figure of Katrina Mulligan had descended once more into the cellar just a couple of seconds earlier and Rose couldn't shake the fear that the ghost's return was bad news, but she also hated the idea of ever going down into that cellar again.

At the edge of her mind, she was starting to pick up on something else, on something far darker and more dangerous than just another of the several ghosts she'd met so far in her short life.

Something huge was coming.

Something powerful.

Something filled with evil that even now

Rose could sense was starting to rise up from the cellar.

And yet...

And yet Rebecca was down there, and Rose knew that she couldn't be left to deal with the danger alone. She looked at Jonathan again and realized quickly that there was no way she could make him wake up in time, and then she crawled over to the edge of the hatch and peered down into the darkness. In that moment, without knowing how, she began to understand that there were several people in the pub's cellar and that already another presence was trying to force its way through.

"Rebecca?" she called out. "Can you come back out?"

She waited.

Silence.

"Rebecca?"

Still she heard no response.

Once again she swallowed hard, and then she began to inch her way down the slope that led down into the depths beneath the pub.

"It's okay, Jonathan," she said, trying her best to stop herself sounding too scared. "Don't be worried when you open your eyes. I just need to make sure that Rebecca's safe. I don't think she quite understands what she's about to -"

Suddenly losing her grip, she let out a brief

cry as she tumbled forward. Rolling down the slope, she fell into the darkness and finally shot off the side of the ramp, falling through the air for a couple of seconds before crashing down against some partially-filled bin bags that had been left in the corner.

As soon as she was sure that she hadn't hurt herself too badly, she began to sit up. The fall had been sudden and unexpected, and she felt a little flustered, but after a few seconds she realized that she could now sense something new in the cellar, something that was clearly far more dangerous than anything she'd ever encountered before. She waited as she felt this danger spreading throughout the dark space, and already she was starting to realize that something evil seemed to be very slowly leaking into the place.

No, into the *world*.

Clambering to her feet, Rose tried to work out what she should do next. She could hear a girl's voice speaking intermittently up ahead, calling out to someone, and a couple of seconds later she briefly heard the baby starting to cry. And then, before she had a chance to react, she realized that she could see the ghostly figure of Katrina Mulligan walking away into the darkness.

"Wait!" Rose gasped, taking a step forward. "I know who you are!"

Katrina's ghost stopped, but she kept her

back turned to Rose as if she wasn't quite able to turn around.

"Why did you come here again?" Rose asked, unable to believe that she was actually daring to speak to the ghost. "I thought you just wanted your baby and... and you've got that now."

She waited, and slowly the figure turned, revealing one side of her pale and very clearly dead face.

"So you *can* hear me," Rose whispered, fighting the desperate urge to turn around and run away. "I thought you could. But I don't understand, why did you come back here if..."

As her voice trailed off, however, Rose realized that perhaps she might be starting to understand after all. Still watching the dead woman's face, she began to pick up on a sense of determination, and perhaps on some other quality that seemed almost to be... regret. For a few seconds Rose struggled to put all the clues together, but slowly she began to realize exactly why Katrina Mulligan had remained in the cellar for so many years and also why she'd now returned. The dead woman wasn't solely trying to be with her dead child and retrieve him from the depths; instead, she also had a far more selfless reason for lingering in the pub's dark and cold spaces.

"You're guarding something," Rose said softly, still unable to quite comprehend the true scale of everything she was sensing. "You're like a sentry, but why? What are you guarding the cellar *from*?"

The dead woman hesitated, before turning away and slowly starting to disappear into the shadows.

"It's the crack in the floor," Rose added as she finally began to understand. "You're not guarding the cellar from something outside. You're guarding it from something that wants to come through from inside the crack."

CHAPTER TWENTY-EIGHT

AS THE BABY CONTINUED to cry, Jessie held the knife above its chest and tried to find the courage she so desperately wanted. Every single second she imagined plunging the blade's tip into the child's wriggling body, yet every single second she found that she was unable to make the final move. She told herself that she was going to get the job done soon, however, and a moment later she heard someone approaching.

"Taylor," she said, and now her voice was trembling as she turned to him. "I need -"

In that instant she froze as she saw Rebecca standing in the archway.

"Give me the baby," Rebecca said cautiously, keeping her eyes on the child. "Whatever you think you might accomplish down here, it's not going to work. And even if it could, even if somehow you summoned the strength to do something so awful... the price would be way too high."

"You don't understand," Jessie stammered through clenched teeth. "There's something down here that can give me power. I felt it the first time I came in. There was that stupid bitch who touched my belly, but there was something else too... something that's fighting to come into this world."

"The ghost of Katrina Mulligan touched my belly too," Rebecca said, edging closer. "I'm not sure, but I think she was checking us both, to see whether we were pregnant. I think she knew that this cellar is no place for a child. She's been guarding against whatever's trying to break through, and she knows it needs a child's body."

"Don't come any closer!" Jessie hissed.

"So what do you think's going to happen?" Rebecca asked. "Do you think that if you kill the baby, something's going to pop up from that crack and thank you by showering you with gifts? What kind of gifts? Money? Influence? Eternal life?"

"It wants proof," she replied. "Proof that I'll do anything for it. Or... I don't know, maybe it wants to possess the baby. How can I know exactly what it's after? I just feel its power and I know I'll do anything to have power of my own. I've never had any before and I'm sick of being nobody."

"So you want to become a child killer?"

"I want to become something!" Jessie snarled. "I want to be important! I want to matter!"

"But not like this," Rebecca said, edging forward again. "If you hurt that child, you'll never be able to undo the damage you'll be causing. Don't you think Jane's baby deserves a chance to live its own life?"

Jessie opened her mouth to reply, before hesitating for a fraction of a second.

"Her," she stammered finally. "Not it. Her. She's a girl."

"Don't you think *she* deserves a chance to live her own life, then?" Rebecca continued. "I don't think you're a bad person and I don't think you really want to hurt that baby. I think you're just confused, but that's okay. People get confused sometimes and -"

Suddenly a shape rushed out of the shadows and grabbed the baby, pulling her from Jessie's hands and carrying her quickly across the cellar. Shocked, Rebecca saw that somehow Rose had made it down into the cellar and that the girl was now holding the baby tight. A moment later Jessie rushed forward, but Rebecca put out a foot and managed to trip her, sending her clattering to the floor. As the knife fell away, Rebecca quickly kicked it into one of the cracks in the concrete.

"Give her back to me!" Jessie screamed,

starting to get to her feet – only for Rebecca to grab her arms from behind and hold her in place. "She's mine!"

"Did I do the right thing?" Rose gasped.

"You did the right thing," Rebecca told her, struggling to hold on as Jessie tried again to pull away. "Although I've got to say, it was a little risky and foolhardy."

"Oh," Rose replied, before thinking for a moment as she continued to hold the crying baby. "Thank you."

"Let go of me!" Jessie gurgled, reaching in vain for the child. "There's still time! It wants blood!"

"What does?" Rose asked.

"I don't know," Rebecca told her, "but I've got a feeling we should be getting out of here soon. I'm not sure -"

Before she could finish, she realized that Jessie was struggling for breath. Still holding the girl's arms, she looked down and saw that her eyes were almost bulging from their sockets. In that moment she let go and pulled back, and to her horror she watched as Jessie once again dropped to her knees. Clawing at her own throat, she seemed to be struggling to get any air at all into her lungs.

"What's wrong with her?" Rose stammered.

"I don't know," Rebecca replied, trying desperately to think of some way she might be able to help. "I think -"

Suddenly Jessie started laughing, bursting into a series of loud, painful gulps as her mouth twisted to become a kind of mockery of a smile. At the same time her eyes were filled with fear as if on some deeper level she was begging for help, and after a couple more seconds Rebecca began to realize that she only had one option.

"We have to get out of here," she said, turning to Rose. "Get upstairs! Take the baby up and I'll be right behind you!"

As those words left her lips, she heard a shuffling sound and spotted Jane – dazed and bloodied – stumbling through from the other end of the basement.

"Help me!" she yelled at the girl. "Jane, grab Jessie's feet!"

Although she clearly had no idea what was happening, Jane rushed over and did as she was told. Together, she and Rebecca carried Jessie to the stairs while Rose hurried on ahead. Despite Jessie's constant trembles and occasional spasms, they managed to get her all the way up to the top of the staircase before taking her into the bar and setting her down on the floor. Already the girl was struggling a little less, and after a few more seconds she managed to finally take a series of sharp, jagged breaths.

"It's okay," Rose said, holding the baby tight

as she sat in the corner. "I think you're safe now."

"Give her to me!" Jane gasped, rushing over and grabbing the child, lifting her up and looking into her crying face. "Mummy's here," she continued. "Are you hurt? Did anyone hurt her?"

"No," Rebecca said, watching as Jessie continued to catch her breath. "I don't think so. It was close, though."

"Help me!" Jessie called out, before finally sitting up. Tears were streaming down her face as she heard footsteps and turned to see that Taylor had also managed to get out of the basement. "That thing... it was like it was inside me and it was trying to squeeze my throat shut."

"It doesn't seem to be able to reach you up here," Rebecca pointed out, before looking down at the floor. "That means it's not as strong as I feared."

"What is it?" Jane sobbed, still holding her baby. "I don't understand what's going on! What did that thing want with Lucy?"

Rebecca was about to answer when she heard someone calling out. Hurrying to the window, she banged on the glass to get Jonathan's attention. Having woken up, he stared at her for a moment before making his way to the front door, and Rebecca quickly pulled the bolt aside so that he could make his way into the building.

"What happened?" he asked.

"It's okay, everyone's safe," Rebecca told

him. "Whatever's in the basement, it reached out for a moment and tried to take control of Jessie. I think it was looking for a body, maybe for a kind of vessel that would allow it to exist more fully in this world."

"I hate this place," Jane whimpered as tears streamed down her face. "I hated it when we arrived and I hate it now!"

"I'm sorry," Jessie said, getting to her feet and making her way over. "I know you probably hate me, but it was like that thing was in my head. It wanted me to... I don't know, to spill your baby's blood. Then it wanted to take over and sort of... possess me. It was so confusing, but I could feel this power coursing through my body." She took a seat and put her head in her hands. "I think something was holding it back, though. Something was stopping it using all of its power."

"Katrina Mulligan," Rebecca whispered.

She turned to Jonathan.

"She's been guarding the cellar for all these years," she continued. "Even after we freed her dead son, she still returned to do her duty. I think she understands that she's the one who brought that entity into the pub in the first place, and she feels that she has to stay around and try to stop it now. The entity wants a child, something it can take over. Perhaps it needed to kill little Lucy first before it could take her body. I don't know exactly, but we have to make sure that it never gets another chance."

"What's going on down here?" Derek Handley called out, stumbling down the stairs in his Spurs shirt and stopping in the doorway. "What are all these people doing in my pub?" He looked around for a moment before spotting his daughter in the corner. "Where did that baby come from?"

CHAPTER TWENTY-NINE

"A GRANDFATHER," DEREK SAID the following morning, sitting in the corner of the bar area with Lucy on his knee. "Me. A grandfather. I'm not old enough. I'm only forty-two."

"I'm sorry," Jane replied, watching him from the doorway. "I should have told you guys."

"I can't believe we missed it," Elizabeth said, shaking her head. "Jane, how did you manage to hide the fact that you were pregnant from us?"

"It's not like I got a huge belly or anything," the girl admitted. "Didn't you notice I started wearing baggier clothes?"

"I thought that was just a phase you were going through," Elizabeth replied, before stepping closer and putting her arms around her daughter. "I don't care how clever you were, your dad and I should have noticed. I suppose we were just too wrapped up in our own mess to pay attention, but that's going to change from now on."

"Should I..."

Jane hesitated for a moment, watching the baby on her father's knee.

"Should I keep her?" she asked finally. "I was thinking about maybe giving her up for adoption so that she can be looked after properly. It's a miracle I've managed to keep her alive for this long."

"Keep her?" Derek replied, turning to her. "You're not sending this little bundle of joy anywhere. We'll make do, just like we've always made do."

"She can't grow up in a pub, though," Jane pointed out. "After everything that happened last night, we're not actually staying here, are we?"

"We've got a contract with the brewery," her father replied.

"Sure, but they can't make us stick to that," she told him. "Not now we know that there's a literal portal to Hell in the basement!"

"Nothing bothers the brewery," Derek muttered.

"It's not a portal to Hell," Elizabeth said, patting her on the shoulder. "It's just a crack and... a ghost and... I don't know, some kind of mix-up. But we're getting it sorted right now. Your dad's taken the money he was going to use for his next season ticket at White Hart Lane and he's pulled in some favors, and your cousin Greg's down in the basement fixing everything as we speak."

"Fixing it?" Jane asked, furrowing her brow for a moment. "How?"

***

The last of the concrete flowed down into the crack before Greg stepped around and began to level the surface off.

"That's not going to hold it," Rebecca said cautiously, watching from the bottom of the stairs as the two guys finished filling the crack. "Is it?"

"It looks pretty strong to me," Jonathan replied, "and once they've moved the beer up into the room behind the bar, there won't be any need for anyone to ever come down here again."

"But -"

"It's a compromise," he added before she could get another word out. "And for what it's worth, I think it's got a chance of working. Whatever was down there in that crack, it's not as if it spent the past seventy years getting more and more powerful. It seemed fairly weak and it couldn't even keep hold of Jessie when you carried her upstairs. With any luck, the crack's sealed now and that'll be the end of it all. At least until the entity finds some other way into the world."

"This'll work just fine," Greg told them as he stepped back to admire his handiwork. "I've used this stuff before, once it dries you'd need some proper industrial gear to ever get through it. It should keep the damp out, too."

As he and his friend headed up the stairs, Rebecca and Jonathan were left alone in the cellar, staring out at the recently-filled cracks that had once spread all across the floor.

"It seems too neat," Rebecca said finally. "Too easy. How can concrete stop a ghost?"

She waited for a response before turning to her husband.

"I don't get it," she added.

"I'm not sure that thing *was* a ghost," he replied, and now he sounded a little more worried than before.

"Then what was it?"

Again she waited, but she could tell that he was reluctant to give voice to his fears.

"Katrina Mulligan invited something into this cellar," he said finally. "Something she didn't understand. Something that perhaps we can *never* understand. And whatever that thing was, it seemed like it wanted to stick around. So it waited for another child to come down here, for a living child this time. Katrina tried to guard against that possibility but eventually Jane showed up with her hidden pregnancy. And that's when the entity began to reach out and try to get hold of the child, except it clearly couldn't just snatch her away. It had to try to be smart, which suggests that it wasn't as powerful as it wanted to be. Not yet, at least."

"Okay," Rebecca said, "but what you're describing doesn't really sound like any ghost we've encountered before. You make it almost sound more like..."

Now it was her turn to fall silent, and also her turn to worry about the words she wanted to say next.

"We need to do a lot more research," Jonathan pointed out. "A hell of a lot more. And while I'd prefer it if The Saracen's Head was shut and left alone for the rest of time, it's clear that won't be happening. They're still talking about opening on Thursday, believe it or not. Even with a possible demon in the -"

He caught himself just in time.

"Demon?" Rebecca said cautiously.

"That was a slip of the tongue."

"Are you sure?"

"I just got carried away," he suggested. "Having said that, I've got some possible avenues for a lot of new research. Katrina Mulligan clearly tapped into something by accident when she was searching for a way to bring her dead child back to life, and whatever that 'something' might be, it still exists. I find it hard to believe that others haven't strayed into the same territory before."

"Are you suggesting that we might meet this thing again?"

"I'm suggesting that we need to understand more about it," he insisted. "A lot more. And from some quick searches I did online this morning, I've already got a few leads." He pulled out his phone and held it up for her to see one of the sites he'd visited. "This one, for example, mentions various entities that might fit the bill."

"Vexaal," she said, reading a few of the names out loud. "Ixial. Ixaal. Those all sound pretty old. They also sound like one of the names Taylor mentioned."

"It's just a theory," he pointed out, as if he was trying in some desperate way to reassure her. "Just because we're taking the whole thing seriously doesn't mean that you need to panic. Not yet. But I've got to admit, this ghost-hunting lark seems to have taken a slightly more serious turn. If I still had any doubts before we came here, they're definitely gone now."

"What about the little boy?" she asked. "The one with the ball?"

"We've seen no sign of him," he replied. "Just because one ghost story was real doesn't mean they all are. From what I can tell, the ghostly boy was genuinely just a figment of everyone's imaginations. They were so focused on him, they mostly missed the far more worrying situation going on in the cellar. People love a good ghost story but maybe they instinctively shy away from the ones that are more terrifying."

Slipping his phone away, he turned to make his way back up the stairs.

"We'd better get Rose home," he added wearily. "The poor kid's exhausted."

"I'll be up in a moment," she told him.

After waiting for her husband to leave her alone, Rebecca took a step forward across the concrete floor. Looking down at the cracks, for a few seconds she thought back to the fear she'd seen on Jessie's face. The girl had come close to killing little Lucy, and Rebecca felt a shiver run through her bones as she once again wondered exactly what kind of entity had been tentatively reaching up from the crack and exploring the world. Deep down, despite her husband's insistence that the situation was mostly under control, she couldn't shake the feeling that – by filling in the cracks with plaster – they'd at best just put a band-aid on the whole thing.

Even if the entity couldn't get through a crack in the floor of some random pub, then what was to stop it eventually finding a way through somewhere else?

"Are you still down there?" she asked finally. "If you are, I hope you realize that we're going to find out what you are one day. And when we do, we're going to make sure that you never get what you want. I'd never allow that to happen." She paused again for a moment as she felt an unfamiliar strength seeping into her chest. "I'd do anything to stop a thing like you. Even if it cost me my own life."

CHAPTER THIRTY

"THIS IS SO STUPID!" Alicia yelled a couple of weeks later, storming across the landing upstairs. "Why can't I have one moment of privacy in this house?"

A moment later a door slammed shut.

"You know," Jonathan said, sitting at the counter in the kitchen as he looked at the cup of tea he'd just made, "I think I get your point. She *is* starting to act more and more like a teenager."

"We should get that office cleared out so that Rose is able to move into her own bedroom," Rebecca pointed out. "I'm pretty sure that'd help hugely."

"I'll make it a priority," he replied. "By the way, I finally got an email from Derek Handley. Apparently the pub's a success and there's been no further sign of Katrina Mulligan's ghost. It sounds like she's gone off to join her family or... wherever ghosts go when they've finished haunting."

"What about the cellar?"

"The new concrete's still in place and they've moved all the equipment upstairs, so nobody has to go down there much," he explained. "I'm still not too pleased that the place is open, but for now at least the danger seems to have passed. I guess financial considerations sometimes win out over common sense. At least Jessie and Taylor seem to be doing okay now. Hopefully they won't have any long-lasting damage from everything that happened."

He waited for a reply, but now he could once again see a faintly faraway quality in his wife's eyes, as if she was pondering something else entirely.

"I was thinking," he continued, "we should probably get to work on some of those crazier theories. I've been reading up on some candidates for that entity in the pub's cellar, and there are a couple that seem to fit the bill."

"I still don't get why Katrina Mulligan mentioned Alexander," she replied, turning to him. "It doesn't make any sense. It's not logical."

"Says the woman who used an actual spirit board," he reminded her. "There's not much logic in *that*, is there?"

"I suppose I was getting desperate," she admitted as she heard footsteps upstairs again, followed by the sound of Alicia hurrying down to the hallway. "Then again, there might be some kind of scientific basis for the board. Either way, I want to keep testing it out."

"Rose is so annoying," Alicia muttered, charging into the kitchen and making a beeline straight for the fridge. "She's such a child."

"She's only two years younger than you," Rebecca pointed out. "Then again, I suppose that feels like a gulf sometimes. Just try to keep the peace and we'll have Rose in her own bedroom by next weekend."

"It won't make much difference," Alicia sighed, taking out some milk and drinking directly from the carton. "I know she can't help it, but she's always saying these really weird things. I swear there's something not quite right in her head, it's like she doesn't know how to actually talk to people. And when she tries, it just comes out all wrong." She put the carton away and pushed the fridge's door shut. "Mum, Dad, I need my own space. Making me share my room with Rose is totally unfair."

"Just try to put up with the situation until next weekend," Rebecca said with a faint smile. "Thing will be better then, I promise."

"Whatever," Alicia replied, turning to walk

back out of the kitchen.

"Actually, can you hold on for a moment?" Jonathan called after her. "There's something important that your mother and I want to talk to you about."

"What now?" she asked, stopping in the doorway and turning to look at him. "Wait, you're not gonna bring *another* weirdo to live with us, are you? Please, tell me you're not that cruel."

"It's nothing like that," Jonathan said, glancing at Rebecca and seeing that she seemed confused, then turning to his daughter again. "Actually, it's about something from the past. Something we thought maybe we wouldn't ever tell you about but... we both think it's only fair that you should know about him."

"Are you sure?" Rebecca whispered.

"I'm sure," he said firmly. "Alicia, you might want to sit down for this. We want to talk to you about Alexander."

"Who's Alexander?" the girl asked cautiously.

"Alexander was... would have been..."

He hesitated as he tried to find the right words.

"Alexander was your brother," he said finally, feeling an immediate rush of relief. "He died before he could be born, but he existed and it's only fair that you should know about him. He shouldn't be a secret."

"My brother?" she replied, staring at him for a moment before sitting down. Already there were tears in her eyes. "What are you talking about? I didn't know I had a brother."

"Well, you did," Jonathan said as Rebecca sat down next to them both. "And even though you never met him, and we didn't really get to meet him either, I think it's important that we talk about him and acknowledge that he was part of our lives."

***

Far away, in the shuttered cellar of The Saracen's Head, the fixed concrete floor sat in silence. Voices could be heard talking in the bar above, accompanied by the regular sound of feet making their way around the pub, but the cellar itself remained completely undisturbed.

***

"Best Sunday roast in Ladburton," the man said as Jane took several empty, gravy-smeared plates from the table, "and you can quote me on that. Tell your mum I've never had a better Yorkshire pudding in my entire life."

"She'll be chuffed to hear that," Jane replied, balancing several plates on one arm before adding an empty gravy jug. "Do you want to see a dessert menu, Steve?"

"I'm full to bursting," the man replied, placing his hands on his ample belly before taking a moment to think. "Go on, we might as well take a look. I might be able to squeeze something else down the hatch."

As she made her way past the bar, Jane saw that her father was busy pulling some more drinks while waiting for a pint of Guinness to settle.

"Table eight want the same again," she told him.

"Alright, hang on," he muttered. "I've only got two arms."

Smiling, Jane took the plates into the kitchen and set them down. Nearby, her mother and a kitchen assistant were already plating up the next set of roasts. Figuring that she had a minute or two to spare, Jane nipped through into the next room and stopped to check on Lucy.

"How are you doing there?" she asked with a smile. "Is Mummy's little girl happy?"

Gurgling with a big smile, Lucy reached up toward her.

"I'll be taking a break soon," Jane continued. "I know this isn't ideal, but we can make it work for now."

"Jane?" Elizabeth called out. "Service!"

"Back I go," Jane said, leaning down and

kissing Lucy on the forehead before hurrying back through to the kitchen. "I swear I never get five minutes to sit down. And Spurs are playing later so it's not as if Dad'll help with the cleaning up."

"Stop dawdling and get these out to table one," Elizabeth said as Jane made her way back through and picked up two of the plates. "I know I shouldn't complain that we're busy, but my ankles are killing me. Tell your dad that if he thinks he's buggering off upstairs later to watch the football and leaving the rest of us to clear up down here, he's got another thing coming."

"Yes, Mum," Jane replied with a smile, turning and carrying the plates out into the hallway.

Stopping for a moment, she listened to the raucous sound coming from the bar. Against all the odds The Saracen's Head was becoming a big success, and she'd somewhat managed to come around to the idea that – at least for now – she was going to be working in the family business. Sure, she wanted to do something more exciting one day, but she figured she needed to stabilize her life a little, especially since she had Lucy to support. At least her parents had both cut way back on the booze, and she was s imply relieved that she no longer had to go out and scoop her mother off the floor of some rundown rival pub. And sure, her father spent a lot of time watching the football, but fortunately he was no longer downing tins of lager every five minutes. For the first time in years, she felt as if things were actually looking up.

Once she'd carried the plates through to the bar, the hallway stood completely empty for a moment. A nearby door had been left open and Lucy let out another gurgle as she shifted slightly in her crib.

And then, with no warning at all, a solitary little ball slowly rolled out from another room and bumped gently to a halt against the skirting board.

Coming soon

The Haunting of Wrackton Hotel
(The Ghosts of Rose Radcliffe book 6)

Owned by the same family for generations, Wrackton Hotel stands proudly overlooking the English Channel. But something is stirring in the many unoccupied rooms, and a dark secret threatens to burst out in search of revenge.

Drawn to the hotel by claims of ghostly inhabitants, Rebecca and Jonathan soon find themselves hunting for a spirit that seems to be trying to deliver a dark warning. The Wracktons themselves are a secretive and somewhat reclusive family who clearly hate the idea of revisiting the past, yet something in the hotel refuses to stay buried.

Meanwhile Alicia struggles to deal with Rose and decides to strike out on her own. Making friends with some of the locals, she quickly discovers that nothing at the hotel is quite what it seems. And when her two worlds come crashing together, will Alicia make the right choice – or is she doomed to repeat the mistakes of her family's past?

The Haunting of Wrackton Hotel is the sixth book in the *Ghosts of Rose Radcliffe* series, about a team of paranormal investigators and their encounters with the supernatural.

Books in this series

1. The Haunting of Quist House
2. The Haunting of Marlstone Hall
3. The Haunting of Lotham Lodge
4. The Haunting of Oxendon School
5. The Haunting of the Saracen's Head
6. The Haunting of Wrackton Hotel

More coming soon

Also by Amy Cross

1689
(The Haunting of Hadlow House book 1)

All Richard Hadlow wants is a happy family and a peaceful home. Having built the perfect house deep in the Kent countryside, now all he needs is a wife. He's about to discover, however, that even the most perfectly-laid plans can go horribly and tragically wrong.

The year is 1689 and England is in the grip of turmoil. A pretender is trying to take the throne, but Richard has no interest in the affairs of his country. He only cares about finding the perfect wife and giving her a perfect life. But someone – or something – at his newly-built house has other ideas. Is Richard's new life about to be destroyed forever?

Hadlow House is brand new, but already there are strange whispers in the corridors and unexplained noises at night. Has Richard been unlucky, is his new wife simply imagining things, or is a dark secret from the past about to rise up and deliver Richard's worst nightmare? Who wins when the past and the present collide?

Also by Amy Cross

If You Didn't Like Me Then,
You Probably Won't Like Me Now

One year ago, Sheryl and her friends did something bad. Really bad. They ritually humiliated local girl Rachel Ritter, before posting the video online for all to see. After that night, Rachel left town and was never seen again. Until now.

Late one night, Sheryl and her friends realize that Rachel's back. At first they think there's on reason to be concerned, but a series of strange events soon convince them that they need to be worried. On the outside, Rachel acts as if all is forgiven, but she's hiding a shocking secret that soon starts to have deadly consequences.

By the time they understand the full horror of Rachel's plans, Sheryl and her friends might be too late to save themselves. Is Rachel really out for revenge? What does she have in store for her tormentors? And just how far is she willing to go? Would she, for example, do something that nobody in all of human history has ever managed to achieve?

If You Didn't Like Me Then, You Probably Won't Like Me Now is a horror novel about the surprising nature of revenge, about the power of hatred, and about the future of humanity.

Also by Amy Cross

The Soul Auction

"I saw a woman on the beach. I watched her face a demon."

Thirty years after her mother's death, Alice Ashcroft is drawn back to the coastal English town of Curridge. Somebody in Curridge has been reviewing Alice's novels online, and in those reviews there have been tantalizing hints at a hidden truth. A truth that seems to be linked to her dead mother.

"Thirty years ago, there was a soul auction."

Once she reaches Curridge, Alice finds strange things happening all around her. Something attacks her car. A figure watches her on the beach at night. And when she tries to find the person who has been reviewing her books, she makes a horrific discovery.

What really happened to Alice's mother thirty years ago? Who was she talking to, just moments before dropping dead on the beach? What caused a huge rockfall that nearly tore a nearby cliff-face in half? And what sinister presence is lurking in the grounds of the local church?

Also by Amy Cross

American Coven

He kidnapped three women and held them in his basement. He thought they couldn't fight back. He was wrong...

Snatched from the street near her home, Holly Carter is taken to a rural house and thrown down into a stone basement. She meets two other women who have also been kidnapped, and soon Holly learns about the horrific rituals that take place in the house. Eventually, she's called upstairs to take her place in the ice bath.

As her nightmare continues, however, Holly learns about a mysterious power that exists in the basement, and which the three women might be able to harness. When they finally manage to get through the metal door, however, the women have no idea that their fight for freedom is going to stretch out for more than a decade, or that it will culminate in a final, devastating demonstration of their new-found powers.

Also by Amy Cross

The Ash House

Why would anyone ever return to a haunted house?

For Diane Mercer the answer is simple. She's dying of cancer, and she wants to know once and for all whether ghosts are real.

Heading home with her young son, Diane is determined to find out whether the stories are real. After all, everyone else claimed to see and hear strange things in the house over the years. Everyone except Diane had some kind of experience in the house, or in the little ash house in the yard.

As Diane explores the house where she grew up, however, her son is exploring the yard and the forest. And while his mother might be struggling to come to terms with her own impending death, Daniel Mercer is puzzled by fleeting appearances of a strange little girl who seems drawn to the ash house, and by strange, rasping coughs that he keeps hearing at night.

The Ash House is a horror novel about a woman who desperately wants to know what will happen to her when she dies, and about a boy who uncovers the shocking truth about a young girl's murder.

AMY CROSS

Also by Amy Cross

Haunted

Twenty years ago, the ghost of a dead little girl drove Sheriff Michael Blaine to his death.

Now, that same ghost is coming for his daughter.

Returning to the small town where she grew up, Alex Roberts is determined to live a normal, quiet life. For the residents of Railham, however, she's an unwelcome reminder of the town's darkest hour.

Twenty years ago, nine-year-old Mo Garvey was found brutally murdered in a nearby forest. Everyone thinks that Alex's father was responsible, but if the killer was brought to justice, why is the ghost of Mo Garvey still after revenge?

And how far will the real killer go to protect his secret, when Alex starts getting closer to the truth?

Haunted is a horror novel about a woman who has to face her past, about a town that would rather forget, and about a little girl who refuses to let death stand in her way.

AMY CROSS

The Curse of Wetherley House

"If you walk through that door, Evil Mary will get you."

When she agrees to visit a supposedly haunted house with an old friend, Rosie assumes she'll encounter nothing more scary than a few creaks and bumps in the night. Even the legend of Evil Mary doesn't put her off. After all, she knows ghosts aren't real. But when Mary makes her first appearance, Rosie realizes she might already be trapped.

For more than a century, Wetherley House has been cursed. A horrific encounter on a remote road in the late 1800's has already caused a chain of misery and pain for all those who live at the house. Wetherley House was abandoned long ago, after a terrible discovery in the basement, something has remained undetected within its room. And even the local children know that Evil Mary waits in the house for anyone foolish enough to walk through the front door.

Before long, Rosie realizes that her entire life has been defined by the spirit of a woman who died in agony. Can she become the first person to escape Evil Mary, or will she fall victim to the same fate as the house's other occupants?

AMY CROSS

Also by Amy Cross

The Haunting of Quist House
(The Ghosts of Rose Radcliffe book 1)

She wakes up alone in a dark house. She has no memory, no idea who she is or where she came from. Blood runs from a wound on one side of her head. She hears strange sounds coming from one of the rooms upstairs. She still doesn't remember anything, but she's starting to realize the awful truth.

She's trapped inside a haunted house.

Not even knowing her own name, the woman starts searching for clues. The strange sounds continue. Is she truly alone, or are there others in the house? And if there are others, are they friend or foe? After making her first shocking discovery, the woman begins to fear the worst. Time is running out. The doors and windows are sealed shut. Nothing makes sense, but a grandfather clock in the hallway seems to offer clues.

Who is this woman? What was she doing in the house before she lost her memory? And even if she remembers in time, will she be able to stop the evil that lurks in the shadows?

AMY CROSS

Also by Amy Cross

The Haunting of Saward Island

Trying to fix their damaged boat, Jacqui Sinclair and her family stop at a remote island that doesn't appear on any maps. They soon discover the horrifying secret that caused previous generations to hide the island's existence from the rest of the world.

Many years ago, the island was the scene of an unspeakable tragedy. Ever since, a malevolent spirit has been lurking in the long grass, waiting near a bare wooden cross for its chance to gain revenge. For Jacqui and the others, their only hope lies in deciphering the clues left behind at a remote lighthouse, where a skeleton crew once tried and failed to defeat the same evil force.

If they fail, the Sinclairs will meet the same grisly fate that has befallen all those who have made the fatal mistake of setting foot on Saward Island...

AMY CROSS

Also by Amy Cross

13 Nights in Crowford

A murdered woman lingers in the old school, waiting for someone to uncover the identity of her killer. A dying painter arrives in the town and finds himself drawn into a nun's final mission. A hunted man takes refuge in an old seaside hotel but finds more than he bargained for. A man returns home after the war, but what dark secret is he hiding?

On the southern coast of England, the town of Crowford has long had a reputation for ghosts. Some even say that the town is home to more ghosts than people. Almost every part of Crowford is haunted, and to prove that claim, here are thirteen stories about the town's mysterious past – from the days before the town had even been founded, through the years of the English Civil War and the era of the Victorians, and on to the horrors and terrors of the twentieth and twenty-first centuries. Together these stories tell the tales not only of Crowford's inhabitants but also of the town itself.

This omnibus edition collects together, for the first time, 13 standalone titles from the Ghosts of Crowford series

AMY CROSS

BOOKS BY AMY CROSS

1. Dark Season: The Complete First Series (2011)
2. Werewolves of Soho (Lupine Howl book 1) (2012)
3. Werewolves of the Other London (Lupine Howl book 2) (2012)
4. Ghosts: The Complete Series (2012)
5. Dark Season: The Complete Second Series (2012)
6. The Children of Black Annis (Lupine Howl book 3) (2012)
7. Destiny of the Last Wolf (Lupine Howl book 4) (2012)
8. Asylum (The Asylum Trilogy book 1) (2012)
9. Dark Season: The Complete Third Series (2013)
10. Devil's Briar (2013)
11. Broken Blue (The Broken Trilogy book 1) (2013)
12. The Night Girl (2013)
13. Days 1 to 4 (Mass Extinction Event book 1) (2013)
14. Days 5 to 8 (Mass Extinction Event book 2) (2013)
15. The Library (The Library Chronicles book 1) (2013)
16. American Coven (2013)
17. Werewolves of Sangreth (Lupine Howl book 5) (2013)
18. Broken White (The Broken Trilogy book 2) (2013)
19. Grave Girl (Grave Girl book 1) (2013)
20. Other People's Bodies (2013)
21. The Shades (2013)
22. The Vampire's Grave and Other Stories (2013)
23. Darper Danver: The Complete First Series (2013)
24. The Hollow Church (2013)
25. The Dead and the Dying (2013)
26. Days 9 to 16 (Mass Extinction Event book 3) (2013)
27. The Girl Who Never Came Back (2013)
28. Ward Z (The Ward Z Series book 1) (2013)
29. Journey to the Library (The Library Chronicles book 2) (2014)
30. The Vampires of Tor Cliff Asylum (2014)
31. The Family Man (2014)
32. The Devil's Blade (2014)
33. The Immortal Wolf (Lupine Howl book 6) (2014)
34. The Dying Streets (Detective Laura Foster book 1) (2014)
35. The Stars My Home (2014)
36. The Ghost in the Rain and Other Stories (2014)
37. Ghosts of the River Thames (The Robinson Chronicles book 1) (2014)
38. The Wolves of Cur'eath (2014)
39. Days 46 to 53 (Mass Extinction Event book 4) (2014)
40. The Man Who Saw the Face of the World (2014)
41. The Art of Dying (Detective Laura Foster book 2) (2014)
42. Raven Revivals (Grave Girl book 2) (2014)

43. Arrival on Thaxos (Dead Souls book 1) (2014)

44. Birthright (Dead Souls book 2) (2014)

45. A Man of Ghosts (Dead Souls book 3) (2014)

46. The Haunting of Hardstone Jail (2014)

47. A Very Respectable Woman (2015)

48. Better the Devil (2015)

49. The Haunting of Marshall Heights (2015)

50. Terror at Camp Everbee (The Ward Z Series book 2) (2015)

51. Guided by Evil (Dead Souls book 4) (2015)

52. Child of a Bloodied Hand (Dead Souls book 5) (2015)

53. Promises of the Dead (Dead Souls book 6) (2015)

54. Days 54 to 61 (Mass Extinction Event book 5) (2015)

55. Angels in the Machine (The Robinson Chronicles book 2) (2015)

56. The Curse of Ah-Qal's Tomb (2015)

57. Broken Red (The Broken Trilogy book 3) (2015)

58. The Farm (2015)

59. Fallen Heroes (Detective Laura Foster book 3) (2015)

60. The Haunting of Emily Stone (2015)

61. Cursed Across Time (Dead Souls book 7) (2015)

62. Destiny of the Dead (Dead Souls book 8) (2015)

63. The Death of Jennifer Kazakos (Dead Souls book 9) (2015)

64. Alice Isn't Well (Death Herself book 1) (2015)

65. Annie's Room (2015)

66. The House on Everley Street (Death Herself book 2) (2015)

67. Meds (The Asylum Trilogy book 2) (2015)

68. Take Me to Church (2015)

69. Ascension (Demon's Grail book 1) (2015)

70. The Priest Hole (Nykolas Freeman book 1) (2015)

71. Eli's Town (2015)

72. The Horror of Raven's Briar Orphanage (Dead Souls book 10) (2015)

73. The Witch of Thaxos (Dead Souls book 11) (2015)

74. The Rise of Ashalla (Dead Souls book 12) (2015)

75. Evolution (Demon's Grail book 2) (2015)

76. The Island (The Island book 1) (2015)

77. The Lighthouse (2015)

78. The Cabin (The Cabin Trilogy book 1) (2015)

79. At the Edge of the Forest (2015)

80. The Devil's Hand (2015)

81. The 13th Demon (Demon's Grail book 3) (2016)

82. After the Cabin (The Cabin Trilogy book 2) (2016)

83. The Border: The Complete Series (2016)

84. The Dead Ones (Death Herself book 3) (2016)

85. A House in London (2016)

86. Persona (The Island book 2) (2016)

87. Battlefield (Nykolas Freeman book 2) (2016)

88. Perfect Little Monsters and Other Stories (2016)

89. The Ghost of Shapley Hall (2016)

90. The Blood House (2016)

91. The Death of Addie Gray (2016)

92. The Girl With Crooked Fangs (2016)

93. Last Wrong Turn (2016)

94. The Body at Auercliff (2016)

95. The Printer From Hell (2016)

96. The Dog (2016)

97. The Nurse (2016)

98. The Haunting of Blackwych Grange (2016)

99. Twisted Little Things and Other Stories (2016)

100. The Horror of Devil's Root Lake (2016)

101. The Disappearance of Katie Wren (2016)

102. B&B (2016)

103. The Bride of Ashbyrn House (2016)

104. The Devil, the Witch and the Whore (The Deal Trilogy book 1) (2016)

105. The Ghosts of Lakeforth Hotel (2016)

106. The Ghost of Longthorn Manor and Other Stories (2016)

107. Laura (2017)

108. The Murder at Skellin Cottage (Jo Mason book 1) (2017)

109. The Curse of Wetherley House (2017)

110. The Ghosts of Hexley Airport (2017)

111. The Return of Rachel Stone (Jo Mason book 2) (2017)

112. Haunted (2017)

113. The Vampire of Downing Street and Other Stories (2017)

114. The Ash House (2017)

115. The Ghost of Molly Holt (2017)

116. The Camera Man (2017)

117. The Soul Auction (2017)

118. The Abyss (The Island book 3) (2017)

119. Broken Window (The House of Jack the Ripper book 1) (2017)

120. In Darkness Dwell (The House of Jack the Ripper book 2) (2017)

121. Cradle to Grave (The House of Jack the Ripper book 3) (2017)

122. The Lady Screams (The House of Jack the Ripper book 4) (2017)

123. A Beast Well Tamed (The House of Jack the Ripper book 5) (2017)

124. Doctor Charles Grazier (The House of Jack the Ripper book 6) (2017)

125. The Raven Watcher (The House of Jack the Ripper book 7) (2017)

126. The Final Act (The House of Jack the Ripper book 8) (2017)

127. Stephen (2017)

128. The Spider (2017)

129. The Mermaid's Revenge (2017)

130. The Girl Who Threw Rocks at the Devil (2018)

131. Friend From the Internet (2018)

132. Beautiful Familiar (2018)

133. One Night at a Soul Auction (2018)

134. 16 Frames of the Devil's Face (2018)

135. The Haunting of Caldgrave House (2018)

136. Like Stones on a Crow's Back (The Deal Trilogy book 2) (2018)

137. Room 9 and Other Stories (2018)

138. The Gravest Girl of All (Grave Girl book 3) (2018)

139. Return to Thaxos (Dead Souls book 13) (2018)

140. The Madness of Annie Radford (The Asylum Trilogy book 3) (2018)

141. The Haunting of Briarwych Church (Briarwych book 1) (2018)

142. I Just Want You To Be Happy (2018)

143. Day 100 (Mass Extinction Event book 6) (2018)

144. The Horror of Briarwych Church (Briarwych book 2) (2018)

145. The Ghost of Briarwych Church (Briarwych book 3) (2018)

146. Lights Out (2019)

147. Apocalypse (The Ward Z Series book 3) (2019)

148. Days 101 to 108 (Mass Extinction Event book 7) (2019)

149. The Haunting of Daniel Bayliss (2019)

150. The Purchase (2019)

151. Harper's Hotel Ghost Girl (Death Herself book 4) (2019)

152. The Haunting of Aldburn House (2019)

153. Days 109 to 116 (Mass Extinction Event book 8) (2019)

154. Bad News (2019)

155. The Wedding of Rachel Blaine (2019)

156. Dark Little Wonders and Other Stories (2019)

157. The Music Man (2019)

158. The Vampire Falls (Three Nights of the Vampire book 1) (2019)

159. The Other Ann (2019)

160. The Butcher's Husband and Other Stories (2019)

161. The Haunting of Lannister Hall (2019)

162. The Vampire Burns (Three Nights of the Vampire book 2) (2019)

163. Days 195 to 202 (Mass Extinction Event book 9) (2019)

164. Escape From Hotel Necro (2019)

165. The Vampire Rises (Three Nights of the Vampire book 3) (2019)

166. Ten Chimes to Midnight: A Collection of Ghost Stories (2019)

167. The Strangler's Daughter (2019)

168. The Beast on the Tracks (2019)

169. The Haunting of the King's Head (2019)

170. I Married a Serial Killer (2019)

171. Your Inhuman Heart (2020)

172. Days 203 to 210 (Mass Extinction Event book 10) (2020)

173. The Ghosts of David Brook (2020)

174. Days 349 to 356 (Mass Extinction Event book 11) (2020)

175. The Horror at Criven Farm (2020)

176. Mary (2020)

177. The Middlewych Experiment (Chaos Gear Annie book 1) (2020)

178. Days 357 to 364 (Mass Extinction Event book 12) (2020)

179. Day 365: The Final Day (Mass Extinction Event book 13) (2020)

180. The Haunting of Hathaway House (2020)

181. Don't Let the Devil Know Your Name (2020)

182. The Legend of Rinth (2020)

183. The Ghost of Old Coal House (2020)

184. The Root (2020)

185. I'm Not a Zombie (2020)

186. The Ghost of Annie Close (2020)

187. The Disappearance of Lonnie James (2020)

188. The Curse of the Langfords (2020)

189. The Haunting of Nelson Street (The Ghosts of Crowford 1) (2020)

190. Strange Little Horrors and Other Stories (2020)

191. The House Where She Died (2020)

192. The Revenge of the Mercy Belle (The Ghosts of Crowford 2) (2020)

193. The Ghost of Crowford School (The Ghosts of Crowford book 3) (2020)

194. The Haunting of Hardlocke House (2020)

195. The Cemetery Ghost (2020)

196. You Should Have Seen Her (2020)

197. The Portrait of Sister Elsa (The Ghosts of Crowford book 4) (2021)

198. The House on Fisher Street (2021)

199. The Haunting of the Crowford Hoy (The Ghosts of Crowford 5) (2021)

200. Trill (2021)

201. The Horror of the Crowford Empire (The Ghosts of Crowford 6) (2021)

202. Out There (The Ted Armitage Trilogy book 1) (2021)

203. The Nightmare of Crowford Hospital (The Ghosts of Crowford 7) (2021)

204. Twist Valley (The Ted Armitage Trilogy book 2) (2021)

205. The Great Beyond (The Ted Armitage Trilogy book 3) (2021)

206. The Haunting of Edward House (2021)

207. The Curse of the Crowford Grand (The Ghosts of Crowford 8) (2021)

208. How to Make a Ghost (2021)

209. The Ghosts of Crossley Manor (The Ghosts of Crowford 9) (2021)

210. The Haunting of Matthew Thorne (2021)

211. The Siege of Crowford Castle (The Ghosts of Crowford 10) (2021)

212. Daisy: The Complete Series (2021)

213. Bait (Bait book 1) (2021)

214. Origin (Bait book 2) (2021)

215. Heretic (Bait book 3) (2021)

216. Anna's Sister (2021)

217. The Haunting of Quist House (The Ghosts of Rose Radcliffe 1) (2021)

218. The Haunting of Crowford Station (The Ghosts of Crowford 11) (2022)

AMY CROSS

219. The Curse of Rosie Stone (2022)

220. The First Order (The Chronicles of Sister June book 1) (2022)

221. The Second Veil (The Chronicles of Sister June book 2) (2022)

222. The Graves of Crowford Rise (The Ghosts of Crowford 12) (2022)

223. Dead Man: The Resurrection of Morton Kane (2022)

224. The Third Beast (The Chronicles of Sister June book 3) (2022)

225. The Legend of the Crossley Stag (The Ghosts of Crowford 13) (2022)

226. One Star (2022)

227. The Ghost in Room 119 (2022)

228. The Fourth Shadow (The Chronicles of Sister June book 4) (2022)

229. The Soldier Without a Past (Dead Souls book 14) (2022)

230. The Ghosts of Marsh House (2022)

231. Wax: The Complete Series (2022)

232. The Phantom of Crowford Theatre (The Ghosts of Crowford 14) (2022)

233. The Haunting of Hurst House (Mercy Willow book 1) (2022)

234. Blood Rains Down From the Sky (The Deal Trilogy book 3) (2022)

235. The Spirit on Sidle Street (Mercy Willow book 2) (2022)

236. The Ghost of Gower Grange (Mercy Willow book 3) (2022)

237. The Curse of Clute Cottage (Mercy Willow book 4) (2022)

238. The Haunting of Anna Jenkins (Mercy Willow book 5) (2023)

239. The Death of Mercy Willow (Mercy Willow book 6) (2023)

240. Angel (2023)

241. The Eyes of Maddy Park (2023)

242. If You Didn't Like Me Then, You Probably Won't Like Me Now (2023)

243. The Terror of Torfork Tower (Mercy Willow 7) (2023)

244. The Phantom of Payne Priory (Mercy Willow 8) (2023)

245. The Devil on Davis Drive (Mercy Willow 9) (2023)

246. The Haunting of the Ghost of Tom Bell (Mercy Willow 10) (2023)

247. The Other Ghost of Gower Grange (Mercy Willow 11) (2023)

248. The Haunting of Olive Atkins (Mercy Willow 12) (2023)

249. The End of Marcy Willow (Mercy Willow 13) (2023)

250. The Last Haunted House on Mars and Other Stories (2023)

251. 1689 (The Haunting of Hadlow House 1) (2023)

252. 1722 (The Haunting of Hadlow House 2) (2023)

253. 1775 (The Haunting of Hadlow House 3) (2023)

254. The Terror of Crowford Carnival (The Ghosts of Crowford 15) (2023)

255. 1800 (The Haunting of Hadlow House 4) (2023)

256. 1837 (The Haunting of Hadlow House 5) (2023)

257. 1885 (The Haunting of Hadlow House 6) (2023)

258. 1901 (The Haunting of Hadlow House 7) (2023)

259. 1918 (The Haunting of Hadlow House 8) (2023)

260. The Secret of Adam Grey (The Ghosts of Crowford 16) (2023)

261. 1926 (The Haunting of Hadlow House 9) (2023)

262. 1939 (The Haunting of Hadlow House 10) (2023)

263. The Fifth Tomb (The Chronicles of Sister June 5) (2023)
264. 1966 (The Haunting of Hadlow House 11) (2023)
265. 1999 (The Haunting of Hadlow House 12) (2023)
266. The Hauntings of Mia Rush (2023)
267. 2024 (The Haunting of Hadlow House 13) (2024)
268. The Sixth Window (The Chronicles of Sister June 6) (2024)
269. Little Miss Dead (The Horrors of Sobolton 1) (2024)
270. Swan Territory (The Horrors of Sobolton 2) (2024)
271. Dead Widow Road (The Horrors of Sobolton 3) (2024)
272. The Haunting of Stryke Brothers (The Ghosts of Crowford 17) (2024)
273. In a Lonely Grave (The Horrors of Sobolton 4) (2024)
274. Electrification (The Horrors of Sobolton 5) (2024)
275. Man on the Moon (The Horrors of Sobolton 6) (2024)
276. The Haunting of Styre House (The Smythe Trilogy book 1) (2024)
277. The Curse of Bloodacre Farm (The Smythe Trilogy book 2) (2024)
278. The Horror of Styre House (The Smythe Trilogy book 3) (2024)
279. Cry of the Wolf (The Horrors of Sobolton book 7) (2024)
280. A Cuckoo in Winter (2024)
281. The Ghost of Harry Prym (2024)
282. In Human Bonds (The Horrors of Sobolton book 8) (2024)
283. Here & Now (The Duchess of Zombie Street book 1) (2024)
284. Blood & Bone (The Duchess of Zombie Street book 2) (2024)
285. Dust & Rain (The Duchess of Zombie Street book 3) (2024)
286. Hope & Hail (The Duchess of Zombie Street book 4) (2024)
287. Blood of the Lost (The Horrors of Sobolton book 9) (2024)
288. Rust & Burn (The Duchess of Zombie Street book 5) (2024)
289. Red-Eyed Nellie (The Horrors of Sobolton book 10) (2024)
290. Echo of the Dead (The Horrors of Sobolton book 11) (2024)
291. The Haunting of Saward Island (2024)
292. Dead End Town (The Horrors of Sobolton book 12) (2024)
293. End of the World (The Horrors of Sobolton book 13) (2024)
294. The Haunting of Marlstone Hall (The Ghosts of Rose Radcliffe 2) (2024)
295. The Haunting of Lotham Lodge (The Ghosts of Rose Radcliffe 3) (2024)
296. The Haunting of Oxendon School (The Ghosts of Rose... 4) (2024)
297. Ben (2024)
298. The Haunting of the Saracen's Head (The Ghosts of Rose... 5) (2024)
299. Crone Finger (2025)

AMY CROSS

For more information, visit:

www.amycross.com

AMY CROSS

Printed in Great Britain
by Amazon